BOOKS AND CROOKS

AND OTHER PLAYS

PLAY TIME!

Books and Crooks

AND OTHER PLAYS

FOR UPPER KEY STAGE TWO

Julia Donaldson

*illustrated by Kate Pankhurst

MACMILLAN CHILDREN'S BOOKS

First published 2013 by Macmillan Children's Books as *Play Time*

This edition published 2025 by Macmillan Children's Books,
an imprint of Pan Macmillan
The Smithson, 6 Briset Street, London EC1M 5NR
EU representative: Macmillan Publishers Ireland Ltd, 1st Floor,
The Liffey Trust Centre, 117–126 Sheriff Street Upper, Dublin 1 D01 YC43
Associated companies throughout the world

ISBN 978-1-0350-1177-3

Text copyright © Julia Donaldson 2013, 2025
Illustrations copyright © Kate Pankhurst 2025

The right of Julia Donaldson and Kate Pankhurst to be identified as the author and illustrator
of this work has been asserted in accordance with the Copyright, Designs and Patents Act 1988.

1 3 5 7 9 8 6 4 2

A CIP catalogue record for this book is available from the British Library.

Printed and bound in the UK using 100% Renewable Electricity by CPI Group (UK) Ltd

Contents

Author's Note

This is the third of three collections of plays for children, designed to be acted or read aloud at school or at home. All of the ones in this book are suitable for children in top primary or lower secondary school, though in fact there is nothing to stop them being acted by adults in an amateur drama group.

The first three plays are all comedies for small casts. *Top of the Mops* (with four parts) is about the farcical misunderstandings that occur when a teenage boy advertises for a new band member while his mother simultaneously advertises for a cleaner. *Problem Page* (with five parts) explores what happens when three family members follow the advice of Dotty, a magazine's agony aunt. And *Books and Crooks* (with five parts) is set in a library and features two innocent-seeming old ladies who are actually responsible for a series of copy-cat crimes.

The final play, *Persephone*, has twenty-five parts so can be performed by a whole class. It is a dramatization of the Greek myth about the capture of the nature goddess Demeter's daughter by Pluto, the king of the underworld. There are three songs in the play, the tunes and chord symbols of which are displayed at the end of the book.

CLEANER WANTED urgently!

01906
234567

SINGER NEEDED TO JOIN NEW BAND!

PHONE 01906 234567

Top of the Mops

Four parts

Characters

Andy Miller, a teenage boy

Carol Miller, Andy's mum

Doreen Blanket, Spike's mother, a cleaner

Spike, a teenage boy, a singer

[The play is set in the hallway of the Millers' home. There is a window, a front door and three more doors, leading to the kitchen, the studio and the broom cupboard.]

SCENE 1: Wednesday, Early Evening

[Andy is sitting by the phone, with a paper on his lap. He dials a number.]

Andy: Hello, I'd like to put an advert in your paper. 'Singer needed to join new band. Phone 01906 234567.' That's it. OK. Thank you. Goodbye.

Carol: *[coming out of the kitchen, sounding cross]* Andy, the freezer's been unplugged.

Andy: What? Oh, sorry, Mum, I needed to plug my new guitar in somewhere.

Carol: What's wrong with your studio? Do you want me to turn it back into a spare room?

Andy: No, of course not. The studio was just a bit . . . crowded, that's all.

Carol: In other words it was a complete tip, as usual.

Andy: I'm sorry, Mum. I meant to plug the freezer back in.

Carol: Well, it's too late now. You'll just have to have soggy beef burgers and melted ice cream for supper.

Andy: I've said I'm sorry.

Carol: And what's this banana skin doing on the floor?

Andy: I don't know – the can-can, maybe.

Carol: Ha ha, very funny.

Andy: Keep your hair on, can't you?

Carol: How can I, when I get back from work to find the house looking like this?

Andy: Well, it's not all me. What about your bedroom?

Carol: My bedroom is like Buckingham Palace compared with your studio. Now go and tidy it!

Andy: I'll do it later.

Carol: You'll do it now. Why are you always so lazy?

Andy: *[going out of the front door]* I must take after you.

[Carol throws the banana skin at him as he goes out.]

Carol: He's right really. I hate housework.
[She picks up the paper.] What's this? Evening News. Hmmmm.
[She dials a number.] Hello, could I put an advert in, please? 'Cleaner wanted urgently. Phone 01906 234567.' Thank you. Goodbye.

SCENE 2: Saturday Morning

[The phone rings. Andy comes out of the studio to answer it.]

Andy: Hi, Andy Miller here.

Doreen: *[on the phone]* Hello, dear, my name's Doreen Blanket. I'm ringing about the job.

Andy: Oh great! Um . . . have you done this sort of thing before?

Doreen: Oh yes, dear, I've worked for ever so many different people.

Andy: That's good. Who have you been with, then?

Doreen: Let's see . . . The Browns, the Robinsons . . .

Andy: I haven't heard of them.

Doreen: The Stones . . .

Andy: The Stones! Really? That's amazing! Er . . . What sort of stuff do you like doing?

Doreen: I'll do whatever needs doing – as long as it's not too heavy, that is.

Andy: Oh no, we're not into heavy metal or anything.

Doreen: That's good, because I've got a bad back. I can't do a lot of lifting. The last place I worked, they wanted me to lift these heavy metal dustbins.

Andy: [puzzled] Really? How strange.

Doreen: Yes, they were a bit. By the way, there's something I ought to warn you about.

Andy: What's that?

Doreen: I do like to sing.

Andy: Well, I should hope so!

Doreen: You don't mind, then? That's good, because the last people didn't like it at all.

Andy: [suddenly a bit worried] Oh dear. Well, I'd need to hear you of course. Could you come round today? At about two? It's 4 Vernon Gardens, by the way.

Doreen: I'll be there!

Andy: That's great! See you at two then, Doreen.
           Goodbye!

Carol: [coming out of the kitchen] Andy, you haven't
           cleared away the breakfast things.

Andy: OK, OK, I'll do it.

[He goes into the kitchen. The phone rings. Carol answers it.]

Carol: Hello, Carol Miller speaking.

Spike: [on the phone] Oh, hi, my name's Spike. I'm
           phoning about the job.

Carol: How wonderful! Have you done this sort of
           work before, Spike?

Spike: Do you mean with a mic or without?

Carol: With Mike, did you say? No, I don't think we
           need Mike as well. We're not that big, you
           know.

Spike: Who have you got, then?

Carol: Just the one boy, Andy — mind you, that's quite
            enough!

Spike: Is he the drummer or what?

Carol: How did you guess? Yes, he is. I'm afraid he's
            not very tidy — the studio is a terrible mess.

Spike: I don't mind that.

Carol: Oh, you sound wonderful, Mike.

Spike: It's Spike.

Carol: Spike, of course — Mike's the other one, isn't he?

Spike: By the way, I do quite a bit of writing.

Carol: Good for you, Spike! I can tell you're a
            bright lad. Just don't carve your name on the
            furniture, will you? *[She laughs.]*

Spike: *[sounding a bit confused]* No. Er . . . where do you
            live?

Carol: We're at 4 Vernon Gardens. You couldn't come round today, Spike, could you? At about two?

Spike: Sure, I'll be there.

Carol: That's terrific. Goodbye!

SCENE 3: 1.45 p.m.

[The doorbell rings and Carol answers it.]

Carol: Hello! You must be Spike.

Spike: That's right. I'm sorry, I'm a bit early.

Carol: Not at all – I'm just so glad to see you!

Spike: By the way, I forgot to ask what you call yourselves.

Carol: I thought I told you – Miller.

Spike: Just Miller? Do you think that's catchy enough?

Carol: Well, I'm not going to start changing my name –
           not even for you, Spike!

Spike: No, OK. Er . . . where's the studio then?

Carol: The studio? Are you sure you want to start
           there? It's in a terrible state, I'm afraid.

Spike: I don't mind.

Carol: Oh, you wonderful young man! It's that door
           there. And all the stuff you'll need is in this
           cupboard. I'll just pop out to the shops if that's
           all right?

Spike: What, now?

Carol: I won't be long.

Spike: OK, then.

[Carol goes out. Spike opens the broom cupboard.]

Spike: I can't see any mics or anything in here. Maybe they're behind all this cleaning stuff. *[He takes out the Hoover, brooms, mop, etc.]* Oh well, I'll have a look in the studio.

[Spike goes into the studio. Andy comes in through the front door.]

Andy: Amazing! Mum's got the Hoover out for once.

[The doorbell rings and Andy answers it.]

Andy: Oh, hi, are you Doreen?

Doreen: That's me, dear. I see you're all ready for me! Oh, that's a very nice Hoover you've got there. It's the latest model, isn't it?

Andy: I don't know.

Doreen: Where shall I plug it in?

Andy: Hey, you don't need to do that. I thought you were going to sing!

Doreen: Oh, you are a one! I do like a bit of music while I work, I must admit.

Andy: Do you know any blues numbers?

Doreen: No, dear, nothing like that. It's the shows I like. *The Sound of Music*, that's got some lovely songs in it, hasn't it?

Andy: Well, it's not really my scene.

Doreen: Then there's *Oliver!*, of course. 'Where is Love?' – that's my favourite.

Andy: Do you like *Cats*?

Doreen: Not really, dear; they shed their hair all over the furniture, you see.

Andy: *[sounding doubtful]* Yes, well, why don't we go into the studio anyway? Maybe we could try out some Stones songs.

[From the studio comes the faint sound of a guitar being strummed.]

Doreen: It sounds like there's someone in there already.

Andy: Probably my mum. She's always nosing around.

Spike: *[singing softly in the studio]*
Woke up this morning. Never felt so bad . . .

Doreen: She's got a very low voice, hasn't she?

Andy: That's not Mum. *[He looks through the keyhole, then whispers.]* It's a bloke! It must be a burglar!

Doreen: *[Whispering]* You don't say! Shall we go in and tackle him?

Andy: No, he could be dangerous. Look, I'll watch the door while you phone the police.

Doreen: Here – have a broom. *[She hands him a broom, then dials 999.]* Police, please. Hello, we've got a burglar.

[Carol returns with the shopping. She sees Andy with the broom.]

Carol: *[in a loud voice]* Andy, what are you doing?

Andy: Shhhhh!

Doreen: [on the phone] What was that? Where am I calling
           from? 4 Vernon Gardens.

Carol: And what's this woman doing using our phone?

Andy: Shhhhh!

Doreen: Mum, there's a burglar in the studio!

[The door of the studio opens and out comes Spike, carrying two
drumsticks. Andy grabs hold of him.]

Andy: Not so fast! Those are my drumsticks!

Carol: Don't be silly – that's not a burglar, it's the new
           cleaner.

Doreen: [dropping the phone in surprise] No it's not, it's my
           Spike!

Spike: [to Doreen] Mum! What are you doing here?

Carol: Really, Spike, fancy asking your mum round to use the phone the second my back's turned.

Spike: I didn't ask her – I don't know what she's doing here.

Carol: A likely story! And look – you've just left all the cleaning things lying in a heap!

Doreen: What's going on, Spike? How do you know these people anyway? And what do you think you're doing messing their house up like this?

Carol: He's supposed to be cleaning it, not messing it up.

Doreen: [to Andy] So you'd already found someone to do the cleaning! Well, I like that! You could have told me.

Spike: I'm not supposed to be cleaning. I'm supposed to be singing!

Doreen: Well, that makes more sense, I must say. He's got a lovely voice, my Spike. It runs in the family.

Andy: *[letting go of Spike]* Do you like blues?

Spike: Sure.

Carol: What's going on? I don't understand.

Doreen: I think I'm beginning to. Let's go back a bit —
           who put the advert in the paper?

Carol: I did.

Andy: No, I did.

Doreen: So there were two ads — one for a cleaner and
           one for a singer. My son Spike here wanted the
           singing job but you thought he was the cleaner.
           Am I making sense, dear?

Carol: Yes, go on!

Doreen: Well, then I came round to do the cleaning, and
           your Andy tried to get me singing in his studio.

Andy: Only Spike was there already. We thought he
           was a burglar.

Doreen: And we phoned the police – what a hoot!

Carol: I think I get it. There's just one thing that's puzzling me, though.

Doreen: What's that, dear?

Carol: Your face – I feel sure I've seen you before somewhere.

Doreen: I seem to recognize you too. It's going back a bit, though.

Carol: Wasn't it just before I had Andy?

Doreen: And I was expecting Spike.

Carol: That's it!

Doreen: The hospital baby classes!

Carol: Do you remember that plastic doll we had to bath?

Doreen: Weren't you the one who kept on dropping her?

Carol: Yes! And you were the one who was always singing!

Doreen: And do you remember the party after the babies were born?

Carol: Yes, of course! Andy was so red – well, purple, really, like a little wrinkled plum. So sweet!

Andy: Mum, shut up!

Doreen: And poor old Spike had that dreadful nappy rash.

Spike: Stop it, Mum!

Carol: And then Andy was sick all over that woman with the twins.

Andy: Mum!

Spike: It's no good. We'll never stop them now.

Andy: Do you want to come into the studio and try out a couple of songs?

Spike: Good idea.

[*Andy and Spike go into the studio.*]

Carol: You were wonderful – you mopped up all the
          sick!

Doreen: Mrs Mop, that's me! Now, dear, I'm just itching
          to get my hands on your beautiful Hoover.

Carol: You're still wonderful!

Doreen: You don't mind if I sing, do you?

Carol: Not at all. You couldn't clean the cooker as
          well, could you? It's filthy, I'm afraid.

Andy: [*coming out of the studio with Spike*] Hey, Mum,
          there's a police car outside the house.

[*They all go to the hall window and look out.*]

Carol: So there is – and two policemen are getting out
          of it.

Doreen: And a sniffer dog as well — isn't he lovely?

Carol: I wonder where they're going?

Andy: Look, they're coming up the front steps.

Everyone: Oh no!

[There is a loud ring at the bell.]

Problem Page

Five parts

Characters

David, a teenage boy

Mrs Jones, David's mother

Mr Jones, David's father, a teacher

Lucy, a teenage girl, David's schoolmate

Dotty, an agony aunt and writer
  of 'Dear Dotty'

SCENE 1

[David's bedroom. On his desk is his homework and a magazine. David is writing a letter.]

David: Dear Dotty, I am a teenage boy with a big problem. I saw your Problem Page in my mum's magazine and I am writing to see if you can help.

[Mrs Jones comes in. David hides the letter and magazine under his homework.]

David: Mum! Why can't you knock?!

Mrs Jones: Why, what are you up to?

David: Nothing – just my homework. What do you want, anyway?

Mrs Jones: I'm looking for my magazine. Have you seen it?

David: No – I mean, yes! I saw Dad with it. He was getting all excited about the gardening page.

Mrs Jones: Was he indeed? I might have guessed. [*She goes out.*]

David: [*going on with his letter*] My problem is my dad. He's a teacher and he's dead embarrassing. He's so keen all the time. He keeps saying things like 'Wow!' and 'Great stuff!' The worst thing is that I've just started at the school where Dad teaches.

Mr Jones: [*outside the room*] David!

David: Oh no!

[*David hides the letter and magazine again. Mr Jones comes in.*]

Mr Jones: Hi. Wow, Mum was right!

David: What do you mean?

Mr Jones: You're actually doing your homework! What subject?

David: Er . . . History. We're doing the First World War.

Mr Jones: Great stuff! You haven't seen Mum's mag, have you? She's accusing me of walking off with it.

David: No, and I wish you and Mum would stop bugging me.

Mr Jones: OK, OK, keep your hair on. I know – shall I go and look up the First World War on the internet for you?

David: No! I mean, yes! Yes, do!

Mr Jones: Terrific!

[*Mr Jones goes out. David breathes a sigh of relief and goes on with his letter.*]

| David: | I didn't want people at school to give me a hard time about Dad, so I've pretended we're not related. It's worked so far. Luckily he doesn't teach me. Also, we've got a very common name, Jones, which helps. But now I've met a girl who wants to come back to the house. How can I stop her meeting my dad? |

SCENE 2

[Dotty's office. Dotty is writing.]

| Dotty: | You will have to make sure your dad is out when this girl comes round. How about sending him a ticket for an interesting talk? As he's such a keen type he is bound to want to go. But you'd better disguise your handwriting. How about copying a teacher's handwriting?
Good luck!
Dotty. |

SCENE 3

[The kitchen, two weeks later. Mr Jones is eating breakfast and Mrs Jones is reading her magazine. There are two doors, one leading out of the house, the other into the hall. David comes in through the hall door, carrying a letter.]

David: There's a letter for you, Dad!

Mr Jones: Wow, what amazing handwriting! Pass the cornflakes, can you?

David: Here you are. Aren't you going to open it, then?

Mr Jones: Do you know what they had for breakfast in the First World War, David?

David: No, Dad.

Mr Jones: Hard biscuits! Pass the milk, there's a good lad.

David: Here you are. But why don't you open your letter?

Mr Jones: They didn't have fresh milk in the trenches, you know.

David: Look, stop going on about the First World War, Dad. Open your letter!

Mrs Jones: Yes, go on, open it.

[Mr Jones opens the envelope.]

Mrs Jones: What is it?

Mr Jones: A ticket.

Mrs Jones: What for?

Mr Jones: A talk about beetles! Great stuff!

David: Are you going to go, Dad?

Mr Jones: Absolutely! It sounds a must!

David: *[relieved]* Mum, can Lucy come round on Tuesday week?

Mr Jones: Lucy Groves in your year? Nice kid. Pity I'll miss her – that's when this talk is.

David: Oh, that's a shame. Well, I'd better get off to school now.

Mr Jones: I'll give you a lift if you like.

David: No thanks, Dad. *[He goes out of the house.]*

Mrs Jones: *[sounding annoyed]* You never told me you'd sent off for a ticket for this talk.

Mr Jones: I didn't send off for it.

Mrs Jones: Then who sent it to you?

Mr Jones: I've no idea!

Mrs Jones: And why is there only one ticket? What about me? *[She snatches the envelope.]* She's got terrible handwriting, hasn't she?

Mr Jones: What makes you think it's a she?

Mrs Jones: I wasn't born yesterday.

Mr Jones: Well, I'd better be off. I know! I'll jog instead
              of taking the car. I might catch up with
              David.

Mrs Jones: He *will* be thrilled.

Mr Jones: Bye, love!

Mrs Jones: *[coldly]* Goodbye.

*[Mr Jones leaves. Mrs Jones flips through her magazine and finds
the problem page. Then she starts to write a letter.]*

Mrs Jones: Dear Dotty,
              I am worried about my husband. He has
              received a mysterious invitation for a talk
              about beetles. He says he doesn't know who
              it's from, but I can guess. I suspect Miss
              Hill, the History teacher at his school. The
              handwriting looks just like hers. I'm afraid
              they may be secretly meeting. What do you
              think I should do?

SCENE 4

[Dotty's office. She is writing.]

Dotty: Why don't you disguise yourself and follow
         your husband? Then you can see if he really
         is going to this talk, and whether or not he is
         meeting anybody.
         Good luck!
         Dotty.

SCENE 5

*[The evening of the talk. David comes into the kitchen from the
hall. He is wearing his coolest clothes. He looks at his watch, then
opens the hall door and calls out.]*

David: Dad! DAD!

[Mr Jones comes in.]

David: It's five to seven, Dad. You're going to be
         late for your talk.

Mr Jones:	Ah! That all depends. What does it depend on, David?
David:	I don't know, Dad. Get a move on.
Mr Jones:	It depends on the distance I have to travel and the speed at which I travel.
David:	*[opening the house door]* Cheerio, Dad!
Mr Jones:	Time equals distance over speed, you see, David.
David:	We're not at school now, Dad. Just go!
Mr Jones:	OK, beetles, here I come! *[He goes out.]*
David:	Bye! *[He closes the door and breathes a sigh of relief.]*
Mrs Jones:	*[from outside the room]* David!
David:	Yes?
Mrs Jones:	Has Dad gone yet?

David: Yes – at last!

[David looks out of the window. He looks at his watch and then out of the window again. He combs his hair. The doorbell rings. David opens the door. Lucy comes in.]

David: Hi, Lucy!

Lucy: Hi! Guess who I saw on the way here?

David: I don't know, who?

Lucy: Mr Jones!

David: [looking worried] Oh – did he say anything to you?

Lucy: No. He was on the other side of the road, running.

David: Oh, yeah. Yes, he must live round here. We often see him out jogging about this time.

Lucy: That's just like him. He's such a keen type, isn't he?

[Mrs Jones comes in through the hall door. She is wearing a long raincoat, a hat and dark glasses.]

David: *[a bit surprised]* Oh, hi, Mum. This is Lucy.

Lucy: Hello, Mrs Jones.

Mrs Jones: Nice to meet you, Lucy. Sorry I can't stop.

[Mrs Jones slinks across the kitchen.]

David: Why are you wearing that long coat and that funny hat?

Mrs Jones: Didn't you hear the weather forecast? There's going to be heavy rain.

David: Then why have you got sunglasses on?

Mrs Jones: I can't talk now – I'm in a hurry. *[She goes out.]*

Lucy: What does your mum do?

David: She doesn't have a job just now. She used to be a drama teacher.

Lucy: She looks kind of dramatic.

David: *[a bit embarrassed]* Do you want a Coke?

Lucy: Yes please. Is your dad in?

David: Er, no. He's working late.

Lucy: What does he do?

David: He works at the hospital.

Lucy: That's amazing – my mum's a hospital doctor. She probably knows your dad. Is he a doctor too?

David: No. No, he's . . . um . . . a porter. He doesn't have much to do with the doctors.

[There is the sound of Mr Jones whistling outside.]

David: Oh no! Lucy, you go into the sitting room. It's just through there. I'll bring the Cokes through. *[He almost pushes her out of the door. Mr Jones comes in through the other door.]*

David: Dad! What are you doing here? Why aren't you at your talk?

Mr Jones: I left the ticket behind. Ah, there it is! *[He picks it up from the table.]* I'll just get my pen too. I think I left it in the sitting room.

David: *[blocking the hall door in alarm]* No, Dad! You haven't got time! You know, distance over speed and all that.

Mr Jones: You may be right, just this once! All right then, buddy, see you later!

[Mr Jones sprints out of the house. Lucy comes back in.]

Lucy: You're taking a long time!

David: Sorry!

Lucy: I thought I heard you talking to someone.

David: Did you? Oh, well, I had the radio on.

Lucy:	It sounded a bit like Mr Jones.
David:	Er . . . yes, it was Mr Jones. He was on the radio! He was giving a talk about . . . beetles!
Lucy:	*[laughing]* That's just like him! Shall we listen to it?
David:	No, it's finished now. Let's take the Cokes through.

[They take the Cokes and go out of the room.]

SCENE 6

[The kitchen, three weeks later. Mrs Jones is writing a letter.]

Mrs Jones:	Dear Dotty, I wrote to you when I thought my husband was meeting another woman. I took your advice and followed him to a very boring talk about beetles. I was pleased to find there was no other woman. But now my husband has gone mad about beetles. He spends all his free

time going on beetle watches. I hardly ever
see him and when I do he just talks about
beetles. I'm so lonely! What can I do?

SCENE 7

[Dotty's office. She is writing.]

Dotty: If you are lonely, why don't you apply for a
job, or else join a club where you will meet
people. A drama group could be good fun.
Good luck!
Dotty.

SCENE 8

*[The kitchen, four weeks later. Mr Jones has just finished marking
some exam papers. Mrs Jones is learning the lines of her play. A
spade is leaning against the table.]*

Mr Jones: That's the last paper! Lucy Groves has come
top. She's a bright girl.

Mrs Jones:	'I hate you! I hate you!'
Mr Jones:	I beg your pardon?
Mrs Jones:	I'm just going over the lines of my play. Do you want to come to the dress rehearsal tonight?
Mr Jones:	Sorry, no can do. I'm off to dig dung! *[He picks up the spade.]*
Mrs Jones:	Dung? Whatever for?
Mr Jones:	Looking for dung beetles.
Mrs Jones:	I might have guessed.
Mr Jones:	They're quite amazing! They bite into a lump of dung, then they kind of roll it around in their mouths, and then they . . .
Mrs Jones:	I don't think I need to know all this. Could you just test me on my lines before you go?
Mr Jones:	You're on! *[He puts the spade down.]*

Mrs Jones:	*[showing him the book]* It's just this page. Can you act Marco? He's Italian. He's in the Mafia.
Mr Jones:	I like it, I like it! *[He takes the book and reads his part with a very strong Italian accent.]* 'Nobody messes with me.'
Mrs Jones:	'You killed him, didn't you? You and your brother, you killed Carlo.'
Mr Jones:	'Carlo was my enemy. My enemies always die.'
Mrs Jones:	'I hate you, I hate you! I want to kill you, both of you! But not with a gun. That would be too easy. I want to kill you slowly, slowly!'
Mr Jones:	*[In his own voice]* Darling, you're wonderful!
Mrs Jones:	That's not in the play.
Mr Jones:	No, but it's true.

Mrs Jones:	Well, I haven't finished being wonderful yet. We're only half-way down the page.
Mr Jones:	I know, but the dung beetles are calling me.
Mrs Jones:	Oh, off you go then. I need to find myself a costume anyway. I'm supposed to wear a short skirt and a long cloak.
Mr Jones:	Wow! Well, I'll be off!

[He goes out of the house. David comes in through the other door.]

David:	What's for supper, Mum?
Mrs Jones:	You'll have to get something from the chippy. I'm going out soon.
David:	Not again!

[Mrs Jones goes out through the hall door. The bell rings. David opens the door. Lucy comes in.]

Lucy:	Hi, David!

David:	Oh, Lucy! I didn't know you were coming round. *[He suddenly sees the exam papers and quickly puts them under the table, which has a long cloth.]*
Lucy:	What are you doing?
David:	Nothing! I mean, just tidying up.
Lucy:	David, are you all right?
David:	Yes, of course. Why?
Lucy:	It's just that I've been a bit worried about you. You keep rushing off suddenly, at school.
David:	Do I? When?
Lucy:	Like that time Miss Hill had to go to a meeting and Mr Jones took our History class at the last minute. You went all white, and then you went to the toilet and didn't come back.

David: Oh yes. Yes, I just felt a bit ill, but I'm OK now.

Lucy: Are you eating all right?

David: Well, Mum's cooking hasn't been too great recently. What's the big doctor act, anyway? Are you trying to be like your mum?

Lucy: That reminds me, I asked my mum about your dad and she couldn't think who he was.

David: Well . . . he's left the hospital now. He didn't work there for very long.

Lucy: What does he do now?

David: Look, Lucy, I don't want to spend the whole evening talking about our parents. I'm starving. Let's go to the chippy.

Lucy: You go. I'll make some tea.

[David goes out. Lucy looks under the table. She sees the exam papers and crawls under. Enter Mrs Jones. She is wearing a very short skirt.]

Mrs Jones: 'I hate you, I hate you! I want to kill you,
               both of you. But not with a gun. That would
               be too easy.'

[Mr Jones lets himself into the house.]

Mr Jones: *[speaking in Marco's Italian accent.]* You looka
               wonderful, my darling!

Mrs Jones: Thanks. But I can't find a cloak to wear.
               What are you doing here, anyway?

Mr Jones: *[still pretending to be Marco]* I forgot my spade.
               I might need it – to bury Carlo! *[He laughs,
               takes his spade and goes out again.]*

Mrs Jones: 'I want to kill you slowly, slowly! Yes! I
               want to see you suffer.' *[She snatches the table
               cloth from the table and puts it round her shoulders,
               like a cloak. Then she sees Lucy.]*

Mrs Jones: Lucy! Aren't you a bit old for Hide and Seek?

Lucy: Um . . . I just spilt some milk. I was mopping
               it up. Mrs Jones, are you all right?

Mrs Jones: Fine, fine! Never felt better! Must go! Bye!

[Mrs Jones trips out of the back door. Lucy shakes her head. Then she puts the exam papers on the table and starts looking through them. David comes back into the house.]

David: I've got the fish and chips.

Lucy: Is your mum all right, David?

David: She's fine.

Lucy: And your dad — is he Italian?

David: No, he's not. Look, Lucy, can you stop going on about my mum and dad? Change the subject, can't you?

Lucy: All right then. Why were these exam papers under the table?

David: *[going white]* Oh, those! Oh yes! I, er . . . well, I picked them up by mistake at school.

Lucy: But they're Mr Jones's exam papers. You're not even in Mr Jones's science class.

David: No, but I can explain!

Lucy: Are you sure everything's all right at home, David?

David: **STOP GOING ON ABOUT MY HOME!** Look, the fish and chips will be getting cold. Let's eat it in front of the telly.

Lucy: **All right, then.** *[She follows David out of the room, still looking worried.]*

SCENE 9

[Lucy's bedroom. She is writing a letter.]

Lucy: Dear Dotty,
I am worried about a friend of mine, or rather about his parents. His mum wears all these mad clothes and is always rushing about. Now my friend says that her cooking

has gone off. Then when I was in their house I heard her saying she wanted to kill someone slowly. I'm afraid she could be trying to poison him and his dad. I also heard his dad say he was going to bury someone. Now my friend has started stealing things from school. Who can I turn to?

SCENE 10

[Dotty's office. She is writing.]

Dotty: This sounds very odd! Is there a nice teacher at school you could talk to about your worries? Good luck!
Dotty.

SCENE 11

[A school science lab in the lunch hour. Mr Jones is doing an experiment. Lucy comes in.]

Lucy: Mr Jones . . .

Mr Jones:	Hello, Lucy! Wow, it's turned purple! Terrific!
Lucy:	Sorry to interrupt, but I'm a bit worried.
Mr Jones:	We can't have that. What seems to be the problem?
Lucy:	Well, it's about a friend of mine.
Mr Jones:	Someone in the school?
Lucy:	Yes, but I'd rather not tell you his name. He doesn't know I'm here, you see.
Mr Jones:	Let's just call him Master X then, shall we? So what is Master X's problem?
Lucy:	He's been stealing from the school. I think it's because he's got an unhappy home.
Mr Jones:	Tell me about it.
Lucy:	Well, his mother is a bit strange. I think she might be going mad and trying to poison him and his dad.

Problem Page

Mr Jones: Good Heavens! What's the dad like?

Lucy: I think he's Italian. My friend told me he was
             a hospital porter, but I've found out he isn't.
             In fact, I'm pretty sure he does something a
             bit . . . well, sinister.

Mr Jones: **Mr Sinister and Mrs Poisoner? Poor old
             Master X!**

[Mrs Jones comes in. She is wearing a smart suit.]

Mrs Jones: **Where on earth is the Head's office? I'm
             completely lost!**

Mr Jones: Down the stairs, turn right and it's first on
             the left.

Mrs Jones: Hello, Lucy! Must fly! Bye! *[She rushes out.]*

Lucy: That's her!

Mr Jones: Who?

Lucy: My friend's mother! The one I was telling you about.

Mr Jones: No, Lucy, you're mistaken. That was my wife!

Lucy: I don't understand . . .

[David comes in.]

David: Lucy, you are here! Someone said you were, but . . . Dad! I mean, Mr Jones, I mean . . . er, I've got to go – I've got football practice.

Mr Jones: Not so fast, David! You've got some explaining to do. What's this story you've been telling Lucy about Mum trying to poison us?

David: I never said that! What are you on about?

Mr Jones: And about me being a sinister porter?

Lucy: I still don't get it. David, is Mr Jones your dad?

David: *[very embarrassed]* Yes.

Lucy: Why didn't you tell me?

David: I didn't tell anyone! I wanted to keep it quiet. I mean, Dad, you can be a bit . . .

Mr Jones: Yes?

David: Well, a bit . . . you know, over the top. I mean, you're not exactly cool. You're so keen all the time.

Lucy: But that's what's so great about Mr Jones! That's why he's such a good teacher! Sorry, Mr Jones, I hope I'm not embarrassing you.

Mr Jones: Wow! Lucy, I'm blushing!

Lucy: Didn't you realize how popular Mr Jones is, David? Everybody likes him.

Problem Page

David: Do they? Well, I'm sorry for lying to you, Lucy. But it sounds like you've been making up stories too. What's all this about Mum trying to poison me? It sounds like something out of her play.

Lucy: What play?

David: *Hatred*, it was called. Dad and I went to see it.

Mr Jones: Yes, great stuff! 'I hate you! I hate you! I could kill you!' and all the rest of it.

Lucy: But David, you never told me about your mum being in a play.

David: No, well, Mum can be even more embarrassing than Dad.

[Mrs Jones comes rushing in.]

Mr Jones: Ah! The poisoner herself!

[Mrs Jones flings her arms round Mr Jones, then round David, then round Lucy.]

Mrs Jones: I've got it! I've got it!

David: Got what?

Mrs Jones: The job!

David: What job?

Mrs Jones: I'm going to be teaching drama here next
              term!

Mr Jones: Terrific! Great stuff!

Lucy: Congratulations, Mrs Jones.

David: *[to himself]* Oh no!

SCENE 12

[David's bedroom. He is writing.]

David: Dear Dotty . . .

Books and Crooks

Five parts

Characters

Oliver Tremble, librarian at
  Boring-by-Sea Library

Robin Banks, a trainee librarian

Homer Lott, an elderly man

Charity Ball, a sweet-seeming old lady
  who recently joined the library

Crystal Ball, Charity's sister, also a new
  library member

[All the scenes are set in Boring-by-Sea Library.]

SCENE 1

[Robin knocks at the door. Oliver comes out of the kitchen and goes to the door. He has a cup of tea in his hand.]

Oliver: We don't open till ten.

Robin: But I'm Robin Banks!

Oliver: There aren't any banks here to rob. This is a library.

Robin: No, no, no! My name is Robin Banks. I'm the new trainee librarian. I'm here for two weeks.

Oliver: Oh, it's you! Sorry, I forgot you were coming. I'll let you in. [He puts down his tea and unlocks the door.] I'm Oliver Tremble.

Robin: Are you really? I'm all of a tremble too, but that's because it's my first day.

Oliver: No, no! Not 'all of a tremble', Oliver Tremble.
          That's my name.

Robin: Oh, of course – you're the head librarian, aren't
          you?

Oliver: I'm the only librarian. Would you like a cup of
          tea?

Robin: No thanks. I'd like a look round.

Oliver: Well, there's not much to look at really. There
          are the books. Here's the computer. The
          kettle's next door. What else do you need to
          know?

Robin: Let's think. Er . . . do you have many events?

Oliver: Events? Well, now and then someone comes and
          changes a book. Is that what you mean?

Robin: No, I mean events like . . . well, story-telling,
          talks, book clubs . . . er . . . puppet shows.

Oliver: Oh no, nothing like that. This is Boring-by-Sea, you know, not London or New York. It's not a very eventful library.

Robin: Still, it's nice and cosy.

Oliver: Yes, it's so cosy you have to pinch yourself to stay awake.

Robin: Can I do anything?

Oliver: You can put these newspapers on that table if you like.

Robin: Jolly good! *[He puts the papers on the table.]*

Oliver: Are you sure you don't want any tea?

Robin: No thanks. I say, it's ten o'clock. Shall I unlock the door?

Oliver: You are keen, aren't you? All right then, here's the key.

Robin: Thank you, Mr Tremble.

[Robin opens the door. Enter Homer.]

Robin: Good morning.

Homer: It looks like rain to me.

Robin: I'm Robin Banks, the new trainee.

Homer: I'm Homer Lott.

Robin: You're home a lot, are you? Then it must make a
           nice change coming here.

Oliver: No, no, no, his name's Homer Lott. He's always
           in here reading the papers.

Homer: Let's see what sort of a mess the world is in
           today.

[He sits down at the newspaper table.]

Robin: Oh dear, Mr Tremble, some of the books aren't
           in the right order. Shall I sort them out?

Oliver: If you must. Well, Homer, tell us the worst.

Homer: 'Five Hundred Job Losses in Car Factory.' 'More Tax Rises On the Way.'

Oliver: What about the *Boring News*?

Homer: 'Sniffer Dog Bites Policeman.'

Robin: That's not boring.

Oliver: No, no, the *Boring News* is the local paper. This is Boring-by-Sea, don't forget.

Robin: Of course, silly me.

Oliver: What else?

Homer: 'Planners Run out of Money.' 'Mayor Gets Drunk Again.' Just the usual stuff. Hold on, what's this? 'Purple Wool Mystery.'

Homer: All right. *[He reads.]* 'Fifty balls of purple wool were stolen from Hammond's department store yesterday. Store detective I.C.U. Steel says, "I spotted a woman putting the balls of wool into a large shopping bag. She had red hair and dark

---

Books and Crooks   63

glasses. When the woman left the shop I asked her to open her bag. To my surprise the bag was empty." The woman gave her name as Olive Branch and her address as 3 Daisy Drive. Police later found that this address did not exist.'

Robin: That's terrible. Isn't there any good news?

Homer: What about this? 'New Weed Resists All Weed Killers.'

Robin: That's not good news.

Homer: It is for the weed.

[Enter Charity and Crystal. They have white hair and are wearing purple cardigans. They each have a large shopping bag.]

Oliver: Here come those two old dears who joined the library last week. Good morning, ladies.

Charity: Good morning, Mr Tremble.

Oliver: This is Robin Banks, our new trainee.

Charity: So nice to meet you!

Crystal: We do hope you'll be happy here.

Robin: Thank you.

Charity: Are our cards ready yet, Mr Tremble?

Oliver: Yes. I'll just check that everything is OK. Do
           you want to watch what I do, Robin?

Robin: Yes, please!

Oliver: Right! I pass this scanner over the card.

Robin: Just like in the supermarket!

Oliver: And the name and address come up on the
           screen.

Robin: Oh yes, look! Miss Charity Ball, 21 Primrose
           Park.

Charity: That's me!

Oliver: Are the name and address correct?

Charity: Of course. Did you think I'd give you false ones?

Oliver: No, I was just checking. Now, I think I let you take out a book last week.

Charity: Yes, you did. That was so kind of you. Here it is. *100 Knitting Patterns*.

Oliver: Was it any good?

Charity: Oh yes! We've each knitted a cardigan.

Crystal: We're wearing them.

Robin: I say, you are quick workers!

Crystal: Yes, we are.

Robin: That purple colour really suits you both!

Crystal: How nice of you to say so.

Charity: You can have the book back now.

Oliver: Thank you.

Charity: May I choose another one?

Oliver: You can choose six if you like.

Charity: Oh, I think just one will keep us busy. *[She goes to the shelves.]*

Oliver: Now, Robin, do you want to check the other lady's card?

Robin: All by myself? Yes, please! Now, I pass the scanner over the card. There we are! Miss Crystal Ball, 21 Primrose Park.

Crystal: That's me! We're sisters, you see. We've just come to Boring. We moved from the other end of the country, you know.

Oliver: Primrose Park. Where is that exactly?

Crystal: Well, it's rather hard to explain. It's sort of . . . tucked away.

Robin: Did you get a book out last week?

Crystal: I got out two! Here they are.

Robin: *Wigs and Disguises* – that looks interesting.

Crystal: Oh, it was! And so useful too!

Robin: What was the other book?

Crystal: This one. *Great Hoaxes of the World*.

Robin: Was that any good?

Crystal: Oh yes, it was excellent! Can I keep them both
          for another week?

Robin: Yes, that's fine.

Homer: *[still reading the papers]* There are a lot of deaths
          this week.

Crystal: Oh dear, are there?

Homer: Yes. D. Creppit, aged ninety-five.

I. B. Old, aged one hundred and ten.

Foo-Foo the poodle, aged thirteen. Funeral on Wednesday in St Paul's Cathedral.

Robin: A funeral for a poodle?

Homer: This is no ordinary poodle. It's Lady Hammond's poodle. She's mad about animals. You should see her Siamese cats. They've all got diamond collars.

Crystal: Have they? How interesting. We love Siamese cats, don't we, Charity?

Charity: Yes, my dear. They're such a lovely cream colour. Do you have a book about them, Mr Tremble?

Oliver: I'm sure we do. I'll look in the animal section. Here, how about this one?

Charity: *Your Siamese Cat and You* by Isa Blue. That sounds good, doesn't it, Crystal? I'll get it out.

Robin: Oh good! I'm dying to see how this is done.

Oliver: It's easy. Scan the card. Scan the barcode. Then
            stamp in the date the book is due back.

Robin: Can I do that bit?

Oliver: Why not? At this rate I'll be able to retire by
            Christmas.

Robin: *[stamping the book]* December 22nd. There you
            are, Miss Ball. You've got three weeks.

Charity: Oh, we won't need that long. As you said, we're
            very quick workers.

Robin: Are you sure you don't want to get out any
            more books? I see you've both got nice big
            shopping bags. They're both the same, aren't
            they?

Crystal: Yes, they're very handy, aren't they, Charity?

Charity: Yes, my dear. Well, goodbye, Mr Tremble.

Crystal: Goodbye, Mr Banks!

Robin: Goodbye!

Oliver: Goodbye, ladies. Don't do anything I wouldn't
          do!

Crystal: I can't promise that!

[Charity and Crystal go out.]

Robin: What sweet old ladies! I say, Mr Tremble, did I
          do that all right?

Oliver: Brilliant. You deserve a tea break.

Robin: Oh, I don't think I'd better.

Homer: I wouldn't. It says here: 'Tea Destroys the Brain
          Cells'.

SCENE 2: Friday, 8 December

[Robin is in the library. Oliver comes in.]

Oliver: Good morning, Robin. You're early again.

Robin: Good morning, Mr Tremble. Do you notice anything different about me?

Oliver: Yes, you've shaved off your moustache. It suits you.

Robin: I didn't have a moustache. No, I mean my badge.

Oliver: Let's have a look. 'I love my library.' Very nice.

Robin: I'm glad you like it. I've got one for you too. It says, 'Books are cool.'

Oliver: Er, thanks.

Robin: Let me pin it on you. *[He pins the badge on to Oliver.]* That looks great!

Oliver: Where did you get these badges?

Robin: I made them. I've got a kit.

[Enter Homer.]

Robin: Good morning, Mr Lott.

Homer: There's thunder in the air.

Robin: Would you like a badge? How about this one?
          'Your paper, your pal.'

Homer: No, that's a bit too jolly. Are there any others?

Robin: Here's a nice one.

Homer: 'Borrow like there's no tomorrow.' That's good
          advice, you know. I'll have that one.

[Robin pins the badge on to Homer. Homer goes to the newspaper
table.]

Oliver: Well, Homer, let's have it.

Homer: 'Petrol Prices Up Again.'
'Tidal Wave Hits Hungary.'

Robin: But Hungary's inland. It hasn't got any sea.

Homer: It has now.

Oliver: What about the *Boring News*?

Homer: 'Chip Shop Closes.' 'Mayor Steals from Washing Line.' The same old stuff. Hold on, this looks a bit more interesting: 'Shee-Shee Stolen.'

Robin: Who's Shee-Shee?

Homer: One of Lady Hammond's Siamese cats.

Robin: The ones with diamond collars?

Homer: That's it.

Robin: How did that happen?

Homer: I'll read it to you. 'On Wednesday Lady Hammond was out at the funeral of her poodle

Foo-Foo. A woman rang at the bell. She had blonde curly hair and a wart on her nose. Lady Hammond's maid, Miss Maida Pott, opened the door.'

Oliver: That reminds me, it's nearly time for tea. Sorry, Homer – go on.

Homer: 'The woman had a bunch of flowers. She asked Miss Pott about Foo-Foo's funeral. When she found she was too late she started to cry. The woman talked to Miss Pott for half an hour. When she left, Miss Pott found that Shee-Shee the cat was missing. A thief had got into the house by the back door and stolen her. Police think that the thief and the woman were working together.'

Robin: That's terrible.

Oliver: But not all that surprising.

Robin: What do you mean?

Oliver: Never mind.

[Enter Charity and Crystal.]

Oliver: Good morning, ladies. Have you finished *Great Hoaxes of the World*?

Crystal: Yes, thank you. It was excellent! Specially page thirty.

Charity: Page seventeen was very good too.

Robin: Would you like a badge?

Charity: How kind of you.

Robin: How about this one?

Charity: What does it say? I haven't got my reading glasses on.

Robin: 'Why beg when you can borrow?'

Charity: Oh, very good! Yes, please.

Crystal: Do you have another one the same for me?

Robin: No, but these two are nearly the same. This one says, 'Why buy when you can borrow?' and this one says, 'Why steal when you can borrow?'

Crystal: I'll have 'Why borrow when you can steal?'

Robin: No, no, no! You've got it the wrong way round.

Charity: Really, Crystal!

Crystal: So silly of me – I'm sorry, Mr Banks.

Robin: That's all right. Shall I pin the badges on for you?

Charity: Yes, please.

Robin: Oh dear, Miss Ball. You've got some hairs on your nice purple cardigan.

Charity: How strange. I wonder how they got there.

Oliver: Are they cream coloured?

Robin: Yes. How did you guess?

Oliver: I'll tell you later. I must make that pot of tea first.

[*He goes into the kitchen. He takes* Great Hoaxes of the World *with him.*]

Charity: We've finished *Your Siamese Cat and You* too.

Robin: Was it good?

Charity: Oh yes, most interesting.

Robin: What about *Wigs and Disguises*?

Crystal: I think we'll need that a little longer.

Charity: Shall we choose some more books?

Crystal: Yes, my dear.

[*They go to the shelves.*]

Homer: 'Bulgaria Beats England 12–0.' 'Banana Split.'

Robin: I'm not interested in recipes, Mr Lott.

Homer: This isn't a recipe. Banana are a rock group and they've just split up.

Charity: Excuse me, Mr Banks. I'd like to take out this book.

Robin: Certainly, Miss Ball.

Charity: I think it looks most interesting, don't you, Crystal?

Crystal: What book have you chosen, my dear?

Charity: *You and Your Van*.

Crystal: Oh, excellent. Yes, I think that sounds absolutely fascinating. And I've found another book that looks extremely entertaining.

Charity: What's it called, my dear?

Crystal: *Great Forgeries of the World*. Here's my card.

Charity: And here's mine.

Robin: Thank you. I'm getting quite good at this.
            *[He scans the cards and books. He date-stamps the
            books.]* The book is due back on December
            the 29th.

Charity: Oh, I think you'll be seeing us before then.

Crystal: Goodbye, Mr Banks. And thank you for the nice
            badges.

Robin: Goodbye.

[Oliver comes back in with a cup of tea.]

Oliver: Have they gone?

Robin: Yes.

Oliver: Good. I can show you page thirty of *Great
            Hoaxes of the World*. Listen to this: 'In 1934 a
            very rich man died in Paris. On the day of his
            funeral a man came to the house with some
            flowers. The butler told him that he was too late
            for the funeral. The man seemed very sad. He
            stayed on the doorstep a long time, talking to

the butler. After he had gone the butler found that another man had broken in and burgled the house.'

Robin: That's very sad. But why are you telling me about it?

Oliver: Doesn't it remind you of anything?

Robin: Of what?

Oliver: Of Lady Hammond's Siamese cat.

Robin: Shee-Shee?

Oliver: Yes. That's just the way she was stolen.

Robin: So you mean someone copied the crime from this book?

Oliver: Not just someone – Crystal and Charity.

Robin: Mr Tremble! Really! What a thing to say!

Oliver: Well, what book did they get out last time?

Robin: *Your Siamese Cat and You*. But that doesn't prove
          anything!

Oliver: No? And what about the cream hairs on their
          cardigans?

Robin: Well, they said they liked Siamese cats. Maybe
          they've got one. It doesn't have to be Shee-Shee.

Oliver: All right, then, what about the purple cardigans?

Robin: What about them?

Oliver: Don't you remember the purple wool that was
          stolen from Hammond's department store?

Robin: Stop this, Mr Tremble, please! I won't have it!

Oliver: Just listen to page seventeen of *Great Hoaxes*.

Robin: Do I have to?

Oliver: It won't take long. Here we are, page seventeen:
          'In 1922 a store detective saw a woman steal
          some rings. She hid them in one of her gloves.

When the woman left the shop the detective arrested her. But when he looked inside the glove it was empty.'

Robin: I don't understand.

Oliver: This is what happened: after the woman had stolen all the rings she put her glove down on a counter. Then another woman swapped it for hers. They were partners in crime, you see. Just like Charity and Crystal.

Robin: But you couldn't fit fifty balls of wool into a glove.

Oliver: No, but Charity and Crystal have got nice big shopping bags. You could fit a lot of wool into them.

Robin: I'm sorry, Mr Tremble. I just don't believe that those two nice old ladies would do a thing like that.

Oliver: Think how keen they are on *Wigs and Disguises*. What did they get out this time?

Books and Crooks

Robin: A book about driving vans.

Oliver: Anything else?

Robin: Yes. A book called *Great Forgeries of the World*.

Oliver: Aha! Something's brewing. That reminds me,
           there's some more tea in the pot. Would you
           like some?

Robin: No thank you, Mr Tremble. And I do think
           you should cut down on all this tea. Maybe Mr
           Lott's right about it destroying the brain cells.
           It certainly seems to be giving you some funny
           ideas.

SCENE 3: Friday, 15 December

[Robin is in the library. He has some posters. Oliver comes in.]

Oliver: Good morning, Robin.

Robin: Good morning, Mr Tremble. Could I put up one
           or two posters?

Oliver: Posters? What posters?

Robin: Here's one of them.

Oliver: Let's have a look. 'Be a bookworm.' Oh yes,
           very good.

Robin: Then there's this one.

Oliver: Why has it got a rabbit on it?

Robin: Read what it says.

Oliver: 'Burrow a book from your library.' I see. Very
           funny. Where did you get these?

Robin: I made them.

Oliver: Go on, then, stick them up.

[Robin starts to stick up the posters. Enter Homer.]

Oliver: Good morning, Homer.

Books and Crooks   85

Homer: There's black ice on the roads. *[He goes to the newspaper table.]*

Oliver: Come on, Homer. Give us the bad news.

Homer: 'Fingernail Found in Fish Finger.' 'Banana Back Together.'

Robin: That's good news, isn't it?

Homer: Not if you've ever heard their music.

Oliver: And the *Boring News*?

Homer: 'School Kids Miss Panto Treat.'
'Mayor's Dark Secret.'

Oliver: Tell us about that.

Homer: I can't. It's a secret. What's this? 'Forger Steals Van.'

Robin: Oh no!

Homer: Oh yes. *[He reads aloud.]* 'On Wednesday,

Top Gear Van Hire hired out a white van to a woman. She gave her name as Miss Hazel Twig of 94 Wallflower Way. The woman paid in cash and left her driving licence with Top Gear. When she failed to return the van, Top Gear called the police. They found that the banknotes and driving licence were forged. Also, the address was false. They are looking for a woman with an Afro hairstyle and a limp.'

Robin: This is terrible! Mr Tremble, you were right all along! Crystal and Charity are a couple of crooks.

Oliver: You look a bit white, Robin. How about a cup of tea? A nice hot sweet one. They say it's good for shock.

Robin: Really, Mr Tremble! Tea! Is that all you can think about? We must do something!

Oliver: Like what?

Robin: Like phoning the police. I don't know why you didn't do that before.

Oliver: You know me, I'm lazy. Anyway, it wasn't as if Crystal and Charity were the great train robbers. They'd only stolen some balls of wool and a cat.

Robin: You never know what they'll stop at. I'm going to phone the police now.

Oliver: Go on then.

Robin: All right. *[He dials.]* Police, please. Hello, it's Robin Banks from the library. It's about Charity Ball. No, not the police charity ball – no, I don't want tickets for that. She's someone you should look into. You should look into Crystal Ball too. No, I'm not a fortune teller. I wish you'd listen! They're two old ladies, and they stole Shee-Shee. They stole the purple wool too, and the van. No, this isn't a hoax call. They're the hoaxers. Their address? It's 21 Primrose Park . . . You say there's no such address? Well, that proves it! What's that? What do they look like? Well, they've got white hair . . . yes, yes, I know, but she must have been wearing a wig! They've been reading a lot of library books, you see. No, it's not me that's been reading too many library books. All right then, be like that. Goodbye. *[He puts down the phone.]* What is the world coming to?

Homer: It's coming to a sticky end if you ask me.

Oliver: Never mind, Robin, you've done your best. Cheer up – it's your last day today. I've bought some jam tarts and Christmas crackers. We can have a little party just before closing time.

Robin: *[still gloomy]* That's very kind of you, Mr Tremble.

Oliver: I'll write a good report about you for head office. And then after Christmas you'll be at a different library. You'll never have to see the Satanic Sisters again.

Robin: *[cheering up a bit]* I hope not.

[Enter Charity.]

Oliver: Well, talk of the devil!

Robin: Oh dear! I can't face this. Mr Tremble, do you mind if I go and sort out some books?

Oliver: You do that.

Charity: Good morning, Mr Tremble.

Oliver: Good morning, Miss Ball. And where's your sister today?

Charity: Oh, she was feeling rather tired. It's been such a busy week. We've been doing a lot of painting.

Oliver: Have you now? And some driving too?

Charity: How did you guess? Oh, of course, that fascinating book, *You and Your Van*. Most helpful. I've brought it back now. And the other book too.

Oliver: Oh yes, *Great Forgeries of the World*. Was that any good?

Charity: Yes indeed, most, er . . .

Oliver: Inspiring?

Charity: You could say that. Especially page sixty-five.

Oliver: Have you brought back *Wigs and Disguises*?

Charity: My sister still has that. But don't worry, she'll send it back to you.

Oliver: Send it? Can't she bring it in?

Charity: Not really, Mr Tremble. I'm afraid I have some rather sad news for you.

Oliver: Have you?

Charity: Well, it's not sad in a way. You see, we're going abroad.

Oliver: For Christmas?

Charity: Oh no, for longer than that. We have to leave in rather a hurry. We're catching the five o'clock car ferry.

Oliver: What, today?

Charity: That's right. My sister is busy packing.

Oliver: So we won't be seeing you again?

Charity: I'm afraid not. We will miss Boring-by-Sea. It's such a sleepy little place. And Primrose Park is such a nice quiet road.

Oliver: So quiet no one's ever been there.

Charity: What was that, Mr Tremble?

Oliver: Oh, nothing, Miss Ball. Well, I'm sorry you won't be borrowing any more books.

Charity: It's a shame, isn't it? But do you mind if I have a little read here? You have such a good crime section.

Oliver: That's fine.

[Charity goes over to the crime shelves. Robin is sorting out books.]

Charity: Oh, it's you, Mr Banks! You look a bit white. Are you all right?

Robin: Yes, thank you. [He drops a pile of books.]

Charity: Let me help you pick them up. Oh, this one
             looks most interesting. It's just what I've been
             looking for. May I have a little look?

Robin: Er, yes, of course. [He goes to the counter and
             whispers with Oliver.]

Oliver: Well, what's she reading?

Robin: Great Kidnappings of the World.

Oliver: Oh dear, oh dear.

Robin: You don't think . . .

Oliver: Yes, I do. It all fits. They're getting the ferry
             at five o'clock. She's not taking that book out.
             She's finding out all she needs to know now.
             And then she'll go out and . . .

Robin: And kidnap someone?

Oliver: Unless someone stops her.

Books and Crooks   93

Robin: But we've tried telling the police.

Oliver: One of us will have to go out after her.

Robin: Which one?

[The phone rings. Oliver answers it.]

Oliver: Hello, Boring Library. Mr Banks? Yes, he's here.
           It's for you.

Robin: For me? Hello, Robin Banks here. Do we have
           what book? *I Love You*? Who is it by?

[Charity comes to the counter.]

Charity: Thank you so much, Mr Tremble. I'll leave the
           book here, shall I? Well, goodbye, it's been so
           nice knowing you.

Oliver: Goodbye, Miss Ball.

[Exit Charity.]

Robin: [on the phone] Can you hold on a minute, please?

Oliver: It's all right, I'll follow her.

Robin: *[to Oliver]* Do you really trust me to look after the library? I say, that's wonderful, Mr Tremble.

Oliver: I hope I'll be back in time for our little tea party.

Robin: Goodbye then, and good luck!

[Exit Oliver.]

Robin: *[on the phone]* I'm sorry to keep you waiting. I was just saying good spy – I mean goodbye to someone. Now, who did you say wrote *I Love You*? William Harry who? William Harry Mee? No, I'm not asking you to marry me. I thought you said . . . Hello? Hello? They've hung up.

Homer: They say there's an earthquake brewing.

SCENE 4: Late Afternoon the Same Day

[Robin and Homer are in the library. Enter Oliver. He looks worn out.]

Robin: Mr Tremble! I'm so pleased to see you! I was getting worried. How did you get on?

Oliver: Put the kettle on and I'll tell you.

Robin: The tea's all ready. I've put the jam tarts on a plate. Shall I bring it all in here?

Oliver: Good idea.

[Robin goes into the kitchen.]

Homer: Have you seen this? 'Dead Man Appears at His Own Funeral.'

Oliver: Homer, I feel as if I'm at my own funeral. I'm worn out.

Homer: Well, I'll be off then.

Oliver: Have a good weekend. Are you going to see the Christmas lights?

Homer: How can I? They've all fused.

[Exit Homer. Robin comes back with the tea, jam tarts and crackers.]

Robin: Now, Mr Tremble, tell me everything. Please tell me they haven't kidnapped anyone.

Oliver: I don't think they have. But what a lot of babies there are in this town! I'm beginning to wonder if one less would make much difference.

Robin: Where have you been?

Oliver: Everywhere! I've been following Charity about. She's been all over the place.

Robin: Doing what?

Oliver: Gazing into prams and pushchairs.

Robin: Oh no!

Oliver: Oh yes! And saying 'coochy coochy coo' to all the babies. I was sure she was going to snatch one of them, but she didn't. Then at three o'clock she went to a primary school.

Robin: What did she do there?

Oliver: She waited outside with all the mums. She went up to a few kids and started chatting to them. But in the end she went away.

Robin: Where to?

Oliver: To a phone box. She was in there for ages.

Robin: And where were you?

Oliver: Hiding in a doorway.

Robin: Did she see you?

Oliver: I'm afraid so. After about twenty minutes she popped out. 'Oh, I'm so sorry, Mr Tremble,' she said. 'Did you want to use the phone? I've just got one more call to make.'

Robin: Did she say who to?

Oliver: Yes – to a taxi firm, to take her to the ferry port.

Robin: What did you do then?

Oliver: I tried to get a taxi and follow her.
          But I couldn't get one, so I came back here.

Robin: Mr Tremble, you're a hero! You've prevented a
          kidnapping. Have a jam tart.

Oliver: Thanks, I will. Now you tell me how you've got
          on.

Robin: Rather well! It was quiet till about half past
          three. I put some tinsel up round the posters.

Oliver: Very nice too.

Robin: After that it got quite busy.

Oliver: Busy? Boring Library? You must be joking!

Robin: No, I'm not. The phone kept going, and that nice lady from the Schools Library Service came in.

Oliver: What lady?

Robin: The one with the black ponytail.

Oliver: I don't know who you mean.

Robin: You must do. She says she comes here once a month. She did tell me her name. What was it? Oh yes, Holly Hock.

Oliver: I don't know anyone called that. What did she want?

Robin: She'd come to collect the books for the schools.

Oliver: What? What books?

Robin: Oh, lots. But she said it was for lots of schools. That's all right, isn't it?

Oliver: Exactly how many books did this lady take away?

Robin: Er, I'm not quite sure. The phone kept ringing, you see.

Oliver: And who was on the phone?

Robin: Well, a lot of different people.

Oliver: Were they all women?

Robin: How did you guess? The funny thing is, they were all asking me about books we didn't have. One lady wanted *Roof Repairs* by Lee King. Then another one asked for by *Storm at Sea* by Gayle Force. I can't remember all the others. I do think you could ask head office for some more new books, Mr Tremble.

Oliver: And all the time you were on the phone this Holly Hock was taking books off the shelves?

Robin: Yes. But it's all right. She gave me a list of them all.

Oliver: Did you look at it?

Robin: Well, no. You see, the phone kept going after she'd left. And then I was getting the tea things ready.

Oliver: Where is this list?

Robin: It's here.

Oliver: Good heavens! She's walked off with all the crime books! And most of the books on travel. And pets. And home decorating.

Robin: Well, maybe the children are doing projects on those subjects.

Oliver: We're talking about five hundred books. How did she take them away?

Robin: Oh, she had a van.

Oliver: A van, did you say?

Robin: Yes, a very nice one. Quite big. White, with 'Schools Library Service' painted on it.

Oliver: Yes. Over the top of 'Top Gear Van Hire'.

Robin: Oh! Oh no! Oh, Mr Tremble, how terrible! You
          don't think it was . . .

Oliver: Crystal Ball, in one of her 'wigs and disguises'.

Robin: I can't bear this! Please say it's not true!

Oliver: Keep your hair on. It's bad enough when Crystal
          takes hers off and changes it every five minutes.

Robin: But Mr Tremble, we thought it was a kidnap
          they were planning.

Oliver: That's just what they wanted us to think.

Robin: I don't get it.

Oliver: I think I do. They knew we knew what they'd
          been up to. They wanted us to know! They
          were even telling us the page numbers that had
          given them their ideas. So when Charity started
          reading that book about kidnapping she knew
          what we'd think.

Books and Crooks

Robin: You mean she was planning for one of us to follow her?

Oliver: She was planning for me to follow her.

Robin: But how did she know it would be you? It could have been me. If you'd stayed behind, the Schools Library trick wouldn't have worked.

Oliver: That's where the phone call came in.

Robin: Which one?

Oliver: The one that came just before Charity left the library.

Robin: The lady who wanted *I Love You* by William Harry Mee?

Oliver: Yes. Don't you remember, she asked to speak to you?

Robin: So you're saying that was Crystal?

Oliver: I am.

Robin: And what about all those other phone calls?

Oliver: That was Charity in the phone box. She was keeping you busy while her sister loaded up the van.

Robin: Oh Mr Tremble, I'm so sorry! I feel terrible! What will head office say to me?

Oliver: Not as much as they'll say to me. I'm the one who left my post.

Robin: Oh dear, oh dear! We could both lose our jobs!

Oliver: Well, that wouldn't be so bad. We could set up as partners in crime, like Charity and Crystal.

Robin: Mr Tremble, don't!

Oliver: Never mind, let's pull the crackers.

[They pull one, gloomily. Oliver gets the gift.]

Robin: What have you got?

Oliver: A toy van.

[They pull the other one.]

Oliver: What about you?

Robin: A lucky charm. I think it's a Siamese cat.

Oliver: Shall we put the paper hats on?

Robin: All right.

[Still gloomy, they put on the hats. The phone rings.]

Oliver: Hello. Boring Library. Oh, hello, Miss Ball.
            What did you say? 'Joyeux Noel'? What does
            that mean? Oh, I see, it's the French for Happy
            Christmas. So you're in France, are you? What?
            No, I haven't done any Christmas shopping yet.
            You're giving people books, you say? What a
            surprise. What was that? Your sister wants to
            speak to Mr Banks? Here he is. [He hands the
            phone to Robin.]

Robin: Hello . . . What's that? You're writing a book,
         are you? What, both of you? I see, you're not
         using your own name. What name are you using
         then? Oh. Well, fancy that. Goodbye.

Oliver: So they're writing a book. What's it called?

Robin: *Great Book Robberies of the World* by M. T. Shelf.

Persephone

Twenty-five parts

Characters

In the Upper World

Demeter, goddess of nature
Perspehone, Demeter's daughter
Pearl, a sea nymph
Coral, a sea nymph
Zeus, king of the gods
Hera, queen of Mount Olympus
   and Zeus's wife
Hecate, a very old goddess
Apollo, god of sun, music and poetry
Alexis, a peasant boy

Alexis's mother, a peasant
Aphrodite, goddess of love and
   beauty
Athena, goddess of wisdom
Hermes, messenger of the gods
Miller
Farmer 1
Farmer 2
Farmer 3
Farmer 4

In the Underworld

Pluto, god of the Underworld
Cerberus, Pluto's three-headed dog
Nicodemus, Pluto's page boy
Cook
Servant 1
Servant 2
Servant 3

OPENING CHORUS

*[Demeter enters, followed by Alexis and his mother,
the miller and the farmers, who carry fruit and corn.
(Music on page 215.)]*

Demeter, Demeter,

She makes the apples sweeter,

And everywhere Demeter goes

The grass grows longer,

The plants grow stronger

And everything grows and grows.

Demeter, Demeter,

She makes the peaches sweeter,

And everywhere Demeter goes

The corn turns yellow,

The pears turn mellow

And everything grows and grows.

[Persephone enters and takes Demeter's hand.]

The sun shines on the water,

The rain falls on the land

When Demeter and her daughter
Go walking hand in hand.

Demeter, Demeter,
She makes the cherries sweeter,
And everywhere Demeter goes
The roots keep rooting,
The shoots keep shooting
And everything grows and grows.

The countryside looks jolly
In reds and pinks and greens
So it's goodbye melon-cauli,
We're feeling full of beans.

Demeter, Demeter,
She makes the apples sweeter,
And everywhere Demeter goes
The grass grows longer,
The plants grow stronger
And everything grows and grows.

[Demeter leaves the stage and everyone follows.]

SCENE 1: The Sea Nymphs

[A seashore by a meadow. Persephone and the two sea nymphs, Coral and Pearl, are playing tag on the beach.]

Coral: Caught you, Pearl!

Pearl: Caught you, Coral!

Persephone: *[in the meadow]* You can't catch me!

Coral: That's not fair, Persephone.

Pearl: You're supposed to stay on the beach!

Persephone: Why should I? I'm not a sea nymph.

Coral: No, but we are.

Pearl: We can't live away from the sea, remember!

Persephone: *[coming back to the beach]* Oh, all right, but let's play something different. Let's collect seaweed.

Demeter:	*[offstage]* **Persephone! Persephone!**
Coral:	Your mother's calling you, Persephone.
Persephone:	Oh no! Just when I'm enjoying myself. Now I'll have to go and help her make things grow.
Pearl:	That sounds like fun to me.
Persephone:	Not when you have to do it every day.
Demeter:	*[entering]* **Persephone!** I wish you wouldn't wander off like that.
Pearl:	Good morning, Demeter. The flowers are looking lovely today. You must have been working hard.
Demeter:	Thank you, Pearl – yes, I have.
Coral:	Why don't you take the morning off?

Demeter:	*[laughing]* No, Coral, I can't do that. I have to ripen all the apples today. Come on, Persephone.
Persephone:	Oh, Mother, do I have to come?
Coral:	Can't she stay here with us, Demeter?
Persephone:	Please, Mother.
Demeter:	I don't know, Persephone . . . if I let you, you must promise not to—
Persephone:	I know, I know, not to talk to any strangers.
Demeter:	And not to eat any food that anyone offers you.
Persephone:	Oh, Mother, you do go on!
Pearl:	We'll look after her, Demeter.

Demeter: I must say, I'd rather go on my own. Persephone usually eats half the fruit that we ripen.

Persephone: I can't help it, I love fruit. You'll bring me some apples back, won't you?

Demeter: Yes, Persephone, I will. Now, be good and don't wander off.

Persephone: No. Goodbye, Mother.

[Exit Demeter.]

Pearl: Look, here's some of that pretty kind of seaweed. You can have a necklace, Persephone! *[She drapes some seaweed round Persephone's neck.]* There, you look like one of us now!

Coral: I wish I could have a necklace of flowers, like your mother.

Persephone: You can! I know where there are lots of flowers!

Pearl:	But, Persephone, you're supposed to stay with us.
Persephone:	I won't go far!
Coral:	She'll be fine! You sound just like Demeter, the way you go on.
Persephone:	*[wandering off]* See you soon!
Pearl:	I hope she'll be all right.
Coral:	Of course she will! Let's go for a swim till she comes back.

[They run off.]

SCENE 2: The Capture

[A meadow. Enter Persephone, picking the petals off a daisy.]

Persephone:	Tinker, tailor, soldier, sailor, rich man, poor man, beggar man, thief — oh no, I'm going to marry a thief!

[Enter Pluto with Servants 1 and 2.]

Pluto: Good morning, Persephone. *[Persephone looks startled but says nothing.]* Well, don't you have a tongue in your head? Ah, I know, you've been told not to talk to strangers, is that it? But I'm not a stranger. I'm a great friend of your mother, the goddess Demeter, and I'm a god too. My servants will tell you which one.

Servant 1:   He's Pluto.

Servant 2:   The god of the Underworld.

[Persephone backs away.]

Pluto: Don't look so shocked, my dear. The Underworld is a very beautiful place.

Persephone: No it's not, it's a horrible, dark place. I've heard all about it.

Pluto: Now, now, you mustn't believe all the stories you hear.

Persephone:	But there are no flowers there, and no grass!
Pluto:	Maybe not, but we have jewels that are brighter than any flowers. Come and see, and I'll give you some to keep! Wouldn't you like a diamond necklace instead of this seaweed one?
Persephone:	No!
Pluto:	You'd love my pet as well.
Persephone:	Pet? What pet?
Pluto:	Cerberus, my three-headed dog. I can't wait to see his tail wagging when he sees the beautiful princess his master has brought back.
Persephone:	You're not going to bring me back!
Pluto:	*[holding out his hand]* Persephone! I beg you to come with me.

Persephone: No! Go away!

Pluto: Now, now, Persephone, I don't want to
                have to force you. Take my hand.

Persephone: Help! *[She tries to run but the servants block
                her way.]*

Pluto: Seize her!

[The servants do so.]

Persephone: Let go! Help! Pearl! Coral!

Servant 1:   It's no use struggling.

Servant 2:   You're coming with us.

Pluto: Hold her tight, but don't hurt her —
                remember she's going to be your queen.

Persephone: I'm not! Let me go!

Pluto: Take her to my carriage.

[The servants go out with Persephone, who is screaming and struggling. She takes off her seaweed necklace and throws it to the ground. Pluto follows them out.]

SCENE 3: Missing

[The seashore. Enter Coral and Pearl, who carries a shell bracelet.]

Pearl: Persephone! Look what we've got! A bracelet of shells.

Coral: *[snatching the bracelet]* Let me give it to her!

Pearl: That's not fair! I made it. *[She runs after Coral.]*

[Enter Demeter with a basket of apples.]

Coral: Oh, hello, Demeter. Mmm, what lovely looking apples. Can I have one?

Demeter: Yes, of course, help yourselves. But where's Persephone?

Coral:	Oh, she's around somewhere.
Demeter:	What do you mean, 'around'? I can't see her.
Pearl:	She's picking some flowers for us.
Demeter:	What? You let her wander off?
Coral:	We didn't want her to – it was her idea.
Pearl:	You see, we made a seaweed necklace for her, and she wanted to make some flower ones for us.
Demeter:	But I told you to stay with her. You promised!
Pearl:	We tried to stop her.
Coral:	We couldn't follow her. We die if we leave the seashore.
Demeter:	Persephone! Persephone! Where has she got to?

Pearl: We'll search the beach, Demeter.

Demeter: And I'll look in the meadows. Persephone!
                Persephone!

[They all wander off, calling her.]

SCENE 4: The First Clue

*[Evening of the same day. A meadow. Enter Alexis and his
mother, who carries a basket of apples.]*

Alexis: These are the best apples I've ever tasted.

Mother: Don't eat any more or you'll make
                yourself sick.

Alexis: All right, I won't eat them, I'll juggle with
                them.

Mother: Stop that — look, you've dropped them,
                they'll be all bruised now.

Alexis:	*[picking up his apples and spotting Persephone's seaweed necklace]* Look, what's this?
Mother:	It's seaweed – that's strange!

[Enter Demeter.]

Mother:	My goodness, here comes the goddess Demeter. *[She curtsies.]* Greetings, Mother Nature. Alex, stop juggling and get down on your knees.
Demeter:	No, no, let the boy play.
Mother:	Why do you look so sad, madam?
Demeter:	Because I have lost my daughter, Persephone. Have you seen her?
Mother:	No, madam, I'm sorry.
Alexis:	I think I might have heard her.
Mother:	Don't be silly, Alex – he's always making up stories.

Alexis:	It's not a story.
Demeter:	Let the child speak.
Alexis:	Well, when I was climbing an apple tree I thought I heard someone calling for help . . . and there was another sound too.
Demeter:	What was that?
Alexis:	A sort of rattling, rumbling noise – like a carriage.
Mother:	Probably just thunder.
Demeter:	What's that you're carrying, child?
Alexis:	It's some seaweed I found.
Demeter:	Persephone's seaweed necklace! So she has been here. Persephone! Persephone!

[Demeter goes off.]

Persephone   125

Mother:	Poor woman!
Alexis:	I thought you said she was a goddess.
Mother:	She is, but she's a mother too, just like me. Look at the grass she's been walking on — it's all brown and withered.
Alexis:	*[biting an apple]* This apple tastes sour!
Mother:	It must be because Demeter is unhappy.

[They go off.]

SCENE 5: Hecate

[A hillside, with the entrance to a cave. It is growing dark. Enter Demeter with a torch.]

Demeter:	Persephone! Where are you? Perhaps she's hiding in this cave. Persephone!
Hecate:	*[coming out of the cave]* Do I look like Persephone? She's a young girl and I,

Hecate, am an old crone. Oh woe!
Oh misery!

Demeter: What's the matter?

Hecate: Don't ask me that! Can't I make moan
without everyone asking me what the
matter is? Oh woe! Oh despair! Oh
tearing out of hair!

Demeter: Can't you control yourself a bit? I'm not
tearing out my hair and I really do have
something to feel miserable about.

Hecate: Oh good! Then we can make moan
together. Alas, alackaday!

Demeter: It's not day, it's night.

Hecate: So it is. All right then, alas, alackanight!
Well, aren't you going to join in?

Demeter: No, I'm too busy looking for my
daughter. Persephone!

Hecate: You'll never find her. She's probably been eaten by a dragon. Why don't you come into my cave and we can wail together till you are a withered old hag like me!

Demeter: No – I've vowed to take no rest, day or night. I've lit this torch from the fire of the volcano, and it will never go out till Persephone returns.

Hecate: In that case, let me go with you, and we can make moan together on the way.

Demeter: If you insist. Persephone! Persephone!

Hecate: Oh woe! Oh blackest of black beetles!

[They go off together.]

SCENE 6: The Underworld

[The Underworld. There is a table and a throne. Andros is setting the table with a plate, knife, fork, spoon, glass and jug. The cook hovers around fussily.]

Cook: **Is that table set, Andros?**

Andros: **Nearly.**

Cook: **Hurry up with the food, Nicodemus!**

[Enter Nicodemus with a trolley. On it are three plates of food. A loud barking is heard offstage.]

Nicodemus: **That's Cerberus barking! Pluto must be back.**

[Enter Pluto, Persephone, Servants 1 and 2 and Cerberus. Everyone else bows. Cerberus leaps around barking.]

Pluto: **Down, Cerberus! Sit! Well, Persephone, what do you think so far? Do you like my Underworld palace?**

Persephone:	Not much.
Pluto:	What? Didn't you notice all the golden statues? And look, this is your throne — it's covered in emeralds!
Persephone:	I don't want a throne — I'd rather sit on the grass. I want to go home!
Pluto:	Perhaps you don't care for emeralds. But just wait till you see our diamonds. Tell her about them, everyone!

[Pluto and the other Underworld characters sing, to the tune of 'Charlie is My Darling', 'The Underworld Song'. (Music on page 177.)]

> Our diamonds are enormous,
> Enormous, enormous,
> Our diamonds are enormous,
> Oh yes, they are.
> They're big and bright and beautiful,
> They're quite spec-tac-u-lar.
> You really ought to see them.

Persephone:	I'd rather see a star.
Pluto and co.:	Our diamonds are enormous But she'd rather see a star.
Pluto:	*[spoken]* Perhaps she likes sapphires better than diamonds.
Pluto and co.:	Our sapphires are stupendous, Stupendous, stupendous, Our sapphires are stupendous, Oh me, oh my! They must be even bluer than The twinkle in your eye. You really ought to see them.
Persephone:	I'd rather see the sky.
Pluto and co.:	Our sapphires are stupendous But she'd rather see the sky.
Pluto:	*[spoken]* See if you can cheer her up, Cerberus.

[Cerberus jumps up and tries to lick Persephone, who pushes him away.]

Pluto and co.:   Our Cerberus has three heads,

                     Yes, three heads, yes three heads.

                     Our Cerberus has three heads,

                     Upon my word!

                     And each of them barks louder far

                     Than any dog you've heard.

                     You really ought to hear him.

Cerberus: *[vaguely to the same tune]*

                     Woof woof woof woof woof woof woof woof!

Persephone: I'd rather hear a bird.

Pluto and co.:   Our Cerberus has three heads.

                     But she'd rather hear a bird.

Cerberus: *[angry and disappointed]*

                     Woof woof woof woof!

Persephone: Take me home, Pluto. I hate it here.

Pluto:	Come now, Persephone, I'm sure you'll see things differently when you've got a good meal inside you. Cook!
Cook:	Yes, Your Majesty.
Pluto:	What is the first course?
Cook:	Curried snakes' eggs, Your Majesty.
Pluto:	Ah, my favourite.
Persephone:	I don't want any.
Pluto:	Take it away!
Cook:	But, Your Majesty!
Pluto:	You heard what I said. Her ladyship wants to skip the starter. What have we next?
Cook:	Cockroaches in coal dust, Your Majesty.
Pluto:	I really can recommend this!

Persephone:	No! Please! Take it away.
Pluto:	How about something nice and sweet and sticky? What is the dessert, cook?
Cook:	Jellied worms with liquorice sauce, Your Majesty.
Persephone:	That's disgusting!
Pluto:	What would you like then, my dear?
Persephone:	I just want to go home to my mother. [*She starts to cry.*]
Pluto:	Ah now, I think I might be able to help with that.
Persephone:	What? You'll take me back, you mean?
Pluto:	Not exactly . . . Pour your mistress out a glass of Lethe water.
Cook:	Yes, Your Majesty.

Persephone: What's this?

Pluto: It's some special water from one of my
                underground rivers. One sip of it will
                make you forget your mother and the
                world above. Then you can be happy here
                with me.

Persephone: No! I'd rather be sad and remember my
                mother than be happy and forget her!

Pluto: Very well, my dear, I won't force you.
                Come, I'll take you on a guided tour – I
                expect you'll feel hungrier after that. And
                if not, there's always tomorrow . . .

[He leads Persephone out. Servants 1 and 2 follow. The cook,
Nicodemus and Andros are left to clear away the rejected food,
hampered by Cerberus who bounds about, trying to eat it.]

SCENE 7: Apollo

[*The following morning. Enter Apollo. He sings (or recites) 'The Sun, the Sun, the Sun'. (Music on page 182.)*]

Apollo: Who turns the night into day?

            The sun, the sun, the sun!

            Who turns the grass into hay?

            The sun, the sun, the sun!

            Who in heaven do you suppose

            Melts all the dewdrops on the rose,

            Paints all the freckles on your nose?

            The sun, the sun, the sun!

            And you're never going to see

            Anyone hotter than me.

            I'm the sun, the sun, the one and only

            Wonderful, wonderful sun!

[*Enter Demeter and Hecate.*]

Demeter: It's Apollo, the sun god.

Hecate: Oh horrible brightness! Oh hideous light!

Apollo:	Good morning, ladies. What can I do for you? Would you like a suntan or a few freckles, or have you just come to admire me?
Demeter:	No, Apollo, I have come to seek news of my daughter, Persephone.
Hecate:	I keep telling you, she's probably fallen off a cliff.
Demeter:	Do be quiet, Hecate. Apollo, you see everything that happens by day. Tell me, what has happened to Persephone?
Hecate:	She's been pecked by vultures.
Apollo:	No such thing.
Demeter:	So you have seen her! Is she alive?
Apollo:	Certainly, madam, and doing very well for herself. Congratulations.
Demeter:	What do you mean?

Apollo:	Your daughter is seated on a throne beside the ruler of the Underworld.
Demeter:	Pluto!
Hecate:	I knew it!
Apollo:	An excellent match. Allow me to congratulate you in verse. Oh what a conquest! Oh what a catch! Oh what a fortunate, fabulous match! Oh what a triumph! Oh what—
Demeter:	Do stop making up poetry and tell me what happened exactly.
Apollo:	Your daughter was picking flowers in the meadow . . . Pretty maiden Making posies, Picking poppies, Plucking roses . . .
Demeter:	**GET ON WITH IT!**

Apollo:	Pluto spotted her and . . . er, whisked her off to the Underworld.
Demeter:	In other words, he's stolen her. We'll see what the king of the gods has to say about that! Come, Hecate, let's go and complain to Zeus.
Apollo:	I wouldn't do that, madam. There's little use in seeking Zeus . . . that was a good rhyme! Use/Zeus – I must remember that.
Demeter:	Stop rambling! Why can't I get Zeus to rescue Persephone?
Apollo:	Because he wants her to stay in the Underworld.
Demeter:	How could he?
Apollo:	Well, you know Pluto has been looking for an Underworld queen for some time.
Demeter:	No!

Apollo:	Oh yes. He's been making a terrible nuisance of himself, pestering all the goddesses. They kept complaining to Zeus about it. So when Zeus heard that Pluto had settled down at last, he was delighted.
Demeter:	This is terrible!
Hecate:	Oh wringing of hands! Oh gnashing of teeth! Come, Demeter, let's go back to my cave and tear out our hair together.
Demeter:	No! If Zeus won't help me, I'll have to rescue Persephone myself.
Apollo:	Demeter, don't talk nonsense. You'll never find the entrance to the Underworld. In any case, it's guarded by Pluto's three-headed dog, Cerberus.
Demeter:	I'd tackle a thirty-headed dog to get my daughter back. Come on, Hecate, let's go.

Hecate: I'm sorry, Demeter, I can't take any more of your hope and determination. I'm going back to my cave. You can join me there as soon as you give up.

Demeter: That will be never!

[Hecate and Demeter go their separate ways during Apollo's speech.]

Apollo: Poor woman! What sorrow! What bravery! I think I'll make up a poem about it:

She roams through the land,
Her torch in her hand,
Seeking her daughter
Through fire and through water,
Her tears making streaks
On her lily-white cheeks . . .

Oh dear! I'm making myself cry. What about you, ladies? Ladies? They've gone!

[He shrugs and saunters away.]

SCENE 8: Starvation

[Two people bring on a sign saying 'six months later'. Enter Alexis and his mother, looking cold, tired and hungry. The miller enters from the other direction.]

Alexis: I'm cold.

Mother: I know you are, Alexis — everyone is.

Alexis: And I'm hungry too. Why is there no fruit on the trees?

Mother: We must make do without fruit. Look, here comes the miller — maybe he can let us have a little flour to make bread with. Good morning, miller.

Alexis: I'm not a miller any more. All the wheat in my barn is used up.

Alexis: Why don't you get some more?

Miller: I can't. No more will grow.

Mother:	Look at the ground – it's frozen solid.

[Enter Demeter, followed by a group of farmers.]

Farmers:	Help us, Demeter. We're starving. Can you do something?
Mother:	*[down on her knees]* Yes, Mother Demeter, help us! You're the only one who can!
Demeter:	What is it you want?
Farmer 1:	We want the plants to grow again!
Alexis:	We want fruit on the trees!
Miller:	I need wheat for people to make into bread.
Farmer 2:	My chickens want corn.
Farmer 3:	My cows will die without any grass to eat.
Farmer 4:	We'll all die!

All:	Help us, Mother Nature!
Demeter:	I can't help you.
Alexis:	Yes you can! I know you can. Remember all those juicy apples you used to fill the trees with!
Demeter:	Used to, child, but not any more. Not since Pluto stole my daughter away. I've given up my other work while I search for her.
Miller:	Isn't that a bit hard on us?
Demeter:	I couldn't help you even if I tried. I'm so unhappy I've lost my power to make things grow.
Alexis:	I'll help you get Persephone back! I'll fight Pluto.
Demeter:	It's no good. Zeus, the king of the gods, is on his side. He wants Persephone to stay in the Underworld.

Mother:	What? And for the grass to dry?
Miller:	And the corn to shrivel?
Farmer 1:	And the fruit to wither?
Farmer 2:	And the animals to starve?
Farmer 3:	And people to freeze?
Farmer 4:	And all of us to die?
Demeter:	It's no use complaining to me. Why don't you pray to Zeus instead?
Miller:	Yes, we'll do that. Zeus!
All:	Zeus! Bring back the grass! Bring back the corn! Bring back the flowers! Bring back the fruit! Bring back the spring! Bring back the summer! BRING BACK PERSEPHONE!

[The chant grows louder and louder. They repeat it as they march off.]

SCENE 9: Hide and Seek

[In the Underworld. Persephone, laughing, runs onstage and hides behind the curtains. Nicodemus, also laughing, runs on, looking for her. (They are playing Hide and Seek.)]

Nicodemus: Persephone! I know you're here!

Persephone: *[jumping out]* Boo!

[They both laugh. Pluto enters, carrying some Lethe water.]

Nicodemus: Oh, sorry, Your Majesty, we were just . . .

Pluto: Playing Hide and Seek, I know. It's good to hear you laugh, Persephone. I do believe you've come to like the Underworld just a little bit.

Persephone:	The caves and twisty passages are good for Hide and Seek — but I'd still rather be in the open air.
Pluto:	But just one sip of Lethe water could change that!
Persephone:	No, Pluto, I'll never drink that. I don't want to forget my mother.
Pluto:	Then if you'd only eat something. Just a tiny slice of spicy roast mole, perhaps? Or a nice crunchy rock cake? I do so want you to be happy with me.
Persephone:	I know you do, Pluto, and I have grown quite fond of you. But I don't even like your kind of food. If I was going to eat anything, it would be something fresh and simple.
Pluto:	Such as?
Persephone:	Such as a piece of my mother's fruit.

Pluto:	Why didn't you say so before?
Persephone:	I haven't said I'll eat it anyway – I promised my mother I wouldn't eat anything.
Pluto:	I'm sure she wouldn't mind you eating some of her food. What a good idea. Nicodemus!
Nicodemus:	Yes, Your Majesty.
Pluto:	Go to the upper world and pick me some fruit.
Nicodemus:	Yes, Your Majesty. *[Exits.]*
Persephone:	I won't eat it!
Pluto:	I feel sure we can tempt you, Persephone. Now, how about a game of chess? You know how much you love the jewelled chess pieces.
Persephone:	Will you set me free if I win?

Pluto:	*[laughing]* You don't give up, do you?
Persephone:	No, I don't.

[They go off together.]

SCENE 10: Mount Olympus

[Two people come on with a sign saying 'Mount Olympus, Home of the Gods'. There is a table, with five goblets and some grapes on it. Zeus is holding a banquet. Seated at the table are his wife Hera, Apollo, Aphrodite and Athene.]

Zeus:	Some more nectar for you, Athene?
Athene:	Thank you, Zeus, it's delicious.
Zeus:	How about you, Aphrodite? Would you like a top-up?
Aphrodite:	That would be divine.
Hera:	Don't offer me any more, will you – I'm only your wife.

Zeus:	Very well, my dear, I won't. Now then, who else – how about Demeter?
Hera:	You know she never comes to our banquets.
Zeus:	That's true – what's she up to these days?
Apollo:	Looking for Persephone.
Zeus:	Oh dear, not still? It's been six months. I thought she'd have cheered up by now.
Apollo:	Alas, poor goddess, all forlorn, Wand'ring through the fields of corn . . .
Hera:	I hate to interrupt, Apollo, but there aren't any fields of corn any more.
Farmers:	*[off]* Bring back the grass! Bring back the corn!
Zeus:	Oh no, not that again! I can't stand it.
Aphrodite:	Just try and ignore it.

Farmers:	Bring back the flowers! Bring back the fruit!
Zeus:	I can feel one of my headaches coming on.
Athene:	Why don't you shoot a thunderbolt at them? That'll shut them up.
Zeus:	I tried that the other day, and it didn't.
Farmers:	Bring back the spring! Bring back the summer!
Apollo:	Would you like me to go and calm them down with some nice poetry?
Hera:	They don't want poetry, they want food.
Farmers:	BRING BACK PERSEPHONE!
Hera:	Why don't you bring her back, Zeus? Then we'd have a bit of peace.
Zeus:	What do you other goddesses think?

Aphrodite:	No, don't let her free – Pluto will just come pestering me.
Athene:	Or me, more likely.
Aphrodite:	You must be joking!
Hera:	I can't see why he should fancy either of you.
Zeus:	Stop that squabbling, my headache's bad enough as it is.
Farmers:	*[louder]* Bring back the grass! Bring back the corn! Bring back the flowers! Bring back the fruit! Bring back the spring! Bring back the summer! BRING BACK PERSEPHONE!
Zeus:	It's no use, I'm going to have to give in. Where's my messenger? Hermes!

Hermes:	*[racing in]* **At your command!**
Zeus:	**Get those wings flapping. I want you to take a message to Pluto.**
Hermes:	**I go, I go!** *[He races out again.]*
Zeus:	**Come back! I haven't told you what the message is yet.**
Hermes:	*[racing back]* **Sorry.**
Zeus:	**Tell him you've come to take Persephone back to her mother.**
Hermes:	**I go, I go!** *[He races out again.]*
Zeus:	**Come back! I haven't finished!**
Hermes:	*[racing back]* **Sorry!**
Zeus:	**Where was I up to?**
Hermes:	**Take Persephone's mother back to her.**

Zeus:	No, you idiot – take Persephone to her mother – unless she's had anything to eat in the Underworld.
Hermes:	I go, I go! *[He races away, then comes back.]* I've come back.
Zeus:	So I see. That was rather quick, wasn't it?
Hermes:	Well, I haven't been yet. Er . . . do I have to?
Zeus:	Yes, of course. Why?
Hermes:	Well, I have the feeling Pluto's not going to be happy about this. He might be angry with me.
Zeus:	And I might hurl a thunderbolt at you if you don't hurry up and go.
Hermes:	I go, I go! *[He races off.]*
Athene:	Oh no, now Pluto'll be after me again!

Aphrodite:	Me, you mean.

Hera:	Shut up, you two.

Voices:	Bring back Persephone! Bring back Persephone! BRING BACK PERSEPHONE!

Zeus:	*[who has been getting more and more frazzled]* All right, all right! I'm bringing her back!

[The chanting continues and the gods leave, blocking their ears.]

SCENE 11: Escape

[In the Underworld, Pluto and Persephone are playing chess.]

Persephone:	Checkmate!

Pluto:	You've won again! You're too clever for me.

Persephone:	So how about setting me free?

[Cerberus is heard barking in the distance. Nicodemus enters, out of breath, carrying a dried-up pomegranate.]

Nicodemus: Your Majesty . . .

Pluto: Ah, you're back, Nicodemus. What have you brought? Rosy apples? Juicy pears?

Nicodemus: Er . . . no, Your Majesty.

Pluto: What then?

Nicodemus: Just . . . this! *[He holds out the pomegranate.]*

Pluto: What's that supposed to be?

Nicodemus: It's a pomegranate, Your Majesty.

Pluto: A pomegranate? Would you call that a pomegranate, Persephone?

Persephone: Well, it could have been one once, I suppose.

Pluto: You hear that! It could have been one once.
                    And you could have been a sensible young
                    man once, instead of a useless halfwit!

Nicodemus: But, Your Majesty, let me
                    explain . . .

Pluto: Silence!

Persephone: Don't be mean, Pluto. Listen to what he
                    has to say.

Pluto: Very well, just for you. But it had better
                    be good.

Nicodemus: Well, Your Majesty, this was all I could
                    find. All the trees were bare and the plants
                    had died. I couldn't even find a blade of
                    grass.

Pluto: What nonsense is this?

Nicodemus: It's true, Your Majesty. People are saying
                    that Demeter is too sad to make anything
                    grow.

Persephone: Oh no! My poor mother. Pluto, you must
               let me go back to her.

[Cerberus is heard barking wildly.]

Pluto: What's up with Cerberus? I'd better go
               and see. [Exits.]

Nicodemus: I'm sorry, Persephone, I really did try to
               find some nice fresh fruit.

Persephone: It's all right, Nicodemus. I wouldn't have
               eaten it anyway . . . though I do love
               pomegranates.

Nicodemus: I'm sorry this one's so dried up.

Persephone: It might not be so dry inside.

Nicodemus: I'll cut it open. [He does so.]

Persephone: Oh, I'd forgotten what fruit looked like.
               It reminds me so much of my mother!

Nicodemus: Won't you have just a little taste?

Persephone: Well, maybe just a nibble . . . while
Pluto's not here. [She takes a small bite.]
Mmm, I can almost see the upper world.

[Enter Pluto and Hermes, with Cerberus gambolling around
them.]

Hermes: That's some dog you've got there, Pluto.

Pluto: Sorry about that, Hermes. Down,
Cerberus. Are you all right?

Hermes: Yes, just about . . . Actually I'm more
frightened of you than of Cerberus.

Pluto: Why, have you brought me bad news?

Hermes: I'm afraid so.

Pluto: Well, don't just stand there! Tell me what
Zeus has to say.

Hermes: He says you must . . . give Persephone
back.

Persephone: Yes!

Pluto: No! Never! I don't believe it! You're
                making this up, Hermes. How dare you?

Hermes: I knew you'd be angry! It's not my fault,
                I'm just the messenger.

Pluto: So I'm to give up Persephone, just like
                that? Is there no way of avoiding it?

Hermes: Just a moment, there was something . . .
                what was it? Oh yes, that's it. You
                can keep Persephone here if she's had
                anything to eat while she's been with you.

Pluto: I see.

[Persephone looks at Nicodemus and puts her finger to her lips.]

Hermes: Well, has she?

Pluto: I can't lie. She's refused everything I've
                offered her.

Hermes:	*[turning to Persephone]* Then you're to come with me!
Persephone:	When can we go?
Hermes:	Straight away! *[He starts to charge out.]*
Persephone:	Wait a second, I must say goodbye. *[Pluto has his back turned.]* Goodbye then, Pluto. Don't look so sad! Maybe I can come back and visit you . . .
Pluto:	Who do you think you're fooling? Demeter will never let you out of her sight again.
Persephone:	Well, goodbye anyway. All right then, Hermes, I'm ready.
Nicodemus:	Aren't you going to say goodbye to me?
Persephone:	Nicodemus, of course! How could I forget? I'll always remember our games of Hide and Seek.

Hermes: Do come on, Persephone. I'm getting
               itchy feet.

Persephone: All right, let's go!

[Hermes takes her hand and they race out together.]

Nicodemus: Shall I clear the table, Your Majesty?

Pluto: Yes. No, wait! Let me taste a morsel of
               the pomegranate first. It could make
               Persephone feel nearer.

Nicodemus: Yes, Your Majesty.

Pluto: What's this? It's already been cut open.
               Someone's eaten a bit. Was it you?

Nicodemus: No, Your Majesty.

Pluto: Who then? Speak! Was it Persephone?
               [Nicodemus is silent.] It was, wasn't it?

Nicodemus: She just had a mouthful, Your Majesty.
               She can't have eaten more than six seeds.

Pluto:	This changes everything!
Nicodemus:	Where are you going?
Pluto:	After them, of course, and you're coming with me. Persephone has eaten in my kingdom. She's mine forever!

[He goes out, pulling Nicodemus with him.]

SCENE 12: The Judgement

[The seashore. Demeter is wandering around, looking tired. Her torch has gone out but she has not noticed this. Enter Coral and Pearl.]

Coral:	Good morning, Demeter.
Pearl:	Still no sign of Persephone?
Demeter:	No.
Coral:	Don't you ever rest?

Demeter:	No. I will search and this torch will burn until Persephone returns.
Coral:	But your torch isn't burning.
Demeter:	How strange! It's gone out – can Zeus be playing tricks on me?
Pearl:	Look, here's a daisy.
Demeter:	That's impossible.
Coral:	And another one.
Demeter:	I don't understand this.

[Persephone runs onstage.]

Persephone:	Mother!
Demeter:	Persephone! Am I dreaming?
Persephone:	No, it's really me! Zeus sent Hermes to bring me back.

Hermes:	*[entering, laughing]* It felt more like you bringing me! I could hardly keep up, even with the wings on my heels.
Persephone:	*[hugging Demeter]* Oh, it's so good to see the grass again! Nicodemus said it had all died.
Hermes:	It had, but everywhere you tread it's been springing back again.
Pearl:	Persephone! We've missed you so much!
Coral:	Was it terrible in the Underworld?
Persephone:	It wasn't so bad once I got used to it. Pluto was very kind to me.
Demeter:	Kind! How could you call him kind when he stole you away from me?
Persephone:	But he was so lonely, Mother. I helped to cheer him up.
Coral:	What does he look like? Is he very ugly?

Persephone   165

Persephone:	No, he's tall and proud-looking, and he always dresses in fine clothes and jewels.
Pluto:	*[entering, followed by Nicodemus]* Just like this!
Persephone:	Pluto!
Demeter:	What are you doing here!
Pluto:	I have come for Persephone.
Demeter:	No! She belongs here!
Hermes:	Remember Zeus's command, Pluto.
Pluto:	Yes, I do remember Zeus's command. Persephone could return, provided she had eaten nothing.
Hermes:	Well? You told me yourself she had refused everything you offered her.
Pluto:	Everything except this! *[He holds out the pomegranate half.]*

Demeter:	You're making this up, Pluto. I'm sure my daughter wouldn't want such a shrivelled-up pomegranate. Would you, Persephone?
Pluto:	Well, Persephone?
Persephone:	Nicodemus, you told him!
Nicodemus:	I'm sorry, Persephone. I meant to keep it a secret, but I found I couldn't lie to Pluto, and . . . I wanted you back too.
Demeter:	So it's true!
Persephone:	It was only a little nibble. I'm sure it doesn't really count!
Pluto:	Come with me, Persephone.
Demeter:	No, she's staying here.
Zeus:	[entering] What are you trying to do – tear the poor girl in half?

Everyone:	Zeus!
Zeus:	Hermes, have you muddled up my message? It was only Persephone you were supposed to bring back from the Underworld, not Pluto as well.
Pluto:	Persephone is mine! She has eaten with me, and now she must stay with me.
Demeter:	But all she ate was six seeds of a pomegranate – one of my pomegranates!
Zeus:	Persephone, is this true?
Persephone:	Yes, it is.
Zeus:	Very well. For every seed you ate you must spend one month of each year underground with Pluto.
Demeter:	No! I can't part with Persephone again!
Zeus:	Wait – but for the other six months she shall stay here with you.

Demeter:	Am I to lose you for half of every year?
Persephone:	Don't be so sad, Mother. I'll be glad to keep Pluto company.
Pluto:	I'll look after her, Demeter.
Nicodemus:	And she can play Hide and Seek with me.
Persephone:	It won't be so bad next time – you'll know that I'll be coming back.
Demeter:	Very well, Zeus. But when Persephone is away, the plants will die and the seeds will stay buried in the earth. We shall call it winter.
Pearl:	Don't think of that time yet, Demeter – Persephone's six months on earth are only just beginning.
Persephone:	We've got the whole summer to look forward to!

[Farmers, the miller, Alexis and his mother and two Underworld servants enter with flowers, fruit and corn.]

All: Demeter, Demeter,

                     She makes the apples sweeter,

                     And everywhere Demeter goes

                     The grass grows longer,

                     The plants grow stronger

                     And everything grows and grows.

[Enter Hecate, followed by remaining characters.]

Hecate: Can't you turn the jollification down? I can't hear myself moan.

Demeter: Never mind your moaning, Hecate. Persephone's back. Come and celebrate with us.

Hecate: Oh all right, just this once, but I'll have to moan extra hard afterwards to make up for it.

All: Demeter, Demeter,
      She makes the peaches sweeter,
      And everywhere Demeter goes
      The corn turns yellow,
      The pears turn mellow
      And everything grows and grows.

      The sun shines on the water,
      The rain falls on the land
      When Demeter and her daughter
      Go walking hand in hand.

      Demeter, Demeter,
      She makes the cherries sweeter,
      And everywhere Demeter goes
      The roots keep rooting,
      The shoots keep shooting
      And everything grows and grows.

      The countryside looks jolly
      In reds and pinks and greens
      So it's goodbye melon-cauli,
      We're feeling full of beans.

Demeter, Demeter,
She makes the apples sweeter,
And everywhere Demeter goes
The grass grows longer,
The plants grow stronger
And everything grows and grows.

Demeter, Demeter

1. De -

- me - ter,___ De - me - ter,___ She
- me - ter,___ De - me - ter,___ She
- me - ter,___ De - me - ter,___ She
- me - ter,___ De - me - ter,___ She

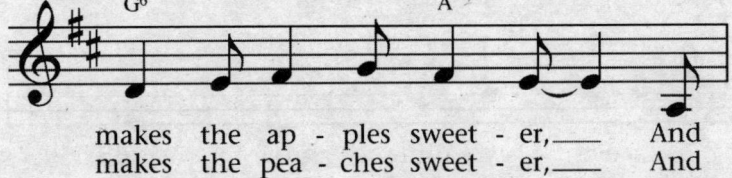

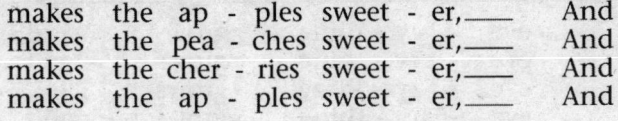

makes the ap - ples sweet - er,___ And
makes the pea - ches sweet - er,___ And
makes the cher - ries sweet - er,___ And
makes the ap - ples sweet - er,___ And

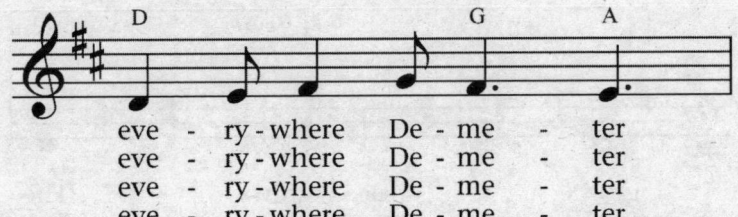

eve - ry - where De - me - ter
eve - ry - where De - me - ter
eve - ry - where De - me - ter
eve - ry - where De - me - ter

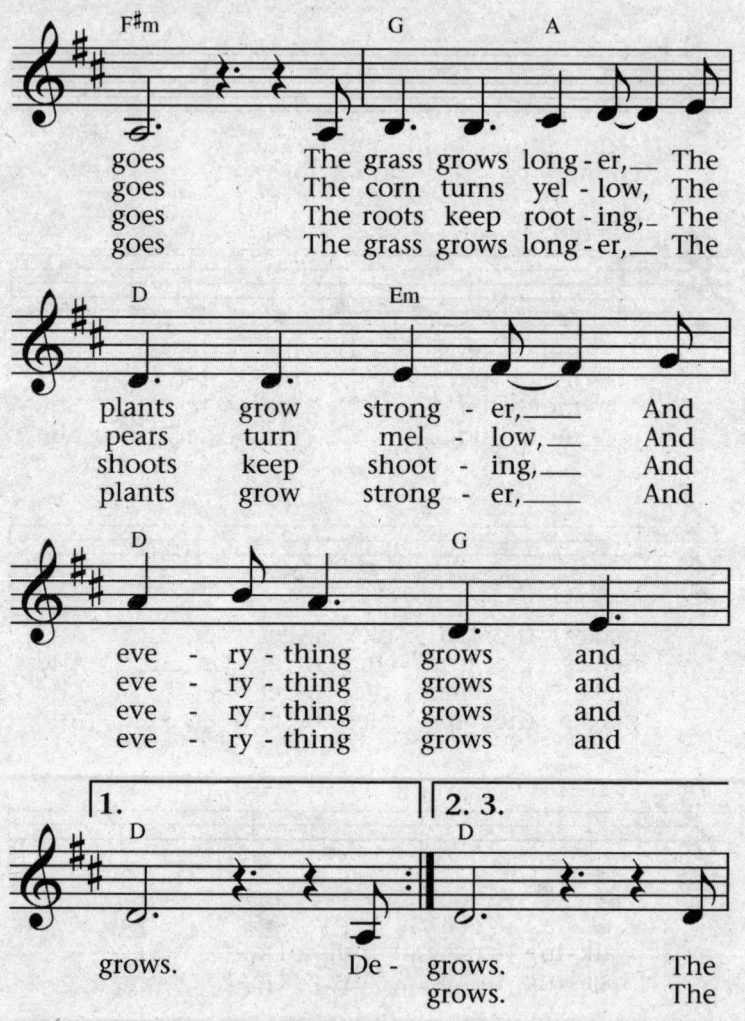

goes   The grass grows long-er,— The
goes   The corn turns yel-low, The
goes   The roots keep root-ing,— The
goes   The grass grows long-er,— The

plants   grow   strong - er,——   And
pears   turn   mel - low,——   And
shoots   keep   shoot - ing,——   And
plants   grow   strong - er,——   And

eve - ry - thing   grows   and
eve - ry - thing   grows   and
eve - ry - thing   grows   and
eve - ry - thing   grows   and

1.
grows.   De -

2. 3.
grows.   The
grows.   The

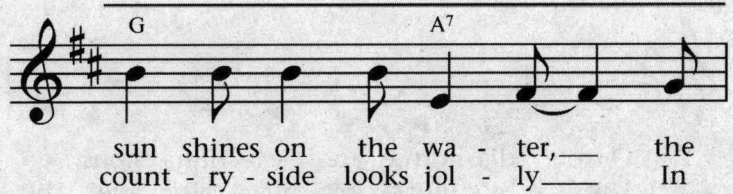

sun shines on the wa - ter,___ the
count - ry - side looks jol - ly___ In

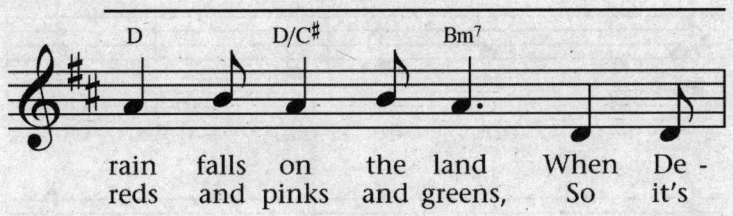

rain falls on the land When De -
reds and pinks and greens, So it's

-me - ter and her daugh - ter___ Go
good - bye me - lon - cau - li,___ We're

walk - ing hand in hand. De - grows.
feel - ing full of beans. De -

The Underworld Song

Our　　dia-monds are　e - nor - mous, e-
Our　　sap-phires are　stu - pen - dous, stu-

-nor - mous, e - nor - mous. Our
-pen - dous, stu - pen - dous. Our

dia - monds are　e - nor - mous, Oh
sap - phires are　stu - pen - dous, Oh

yes, they　　are.　They're big and bright and
me, oh　　my!　They must be　e - ven

beau - ti - ful, They're quite spec - tac - u -
blu - er than the twin - kle in your

-lar.   You real - ly ought to
eye.   You real - ly ought to

see_____ them._ I'd ra - ther see a
see_____ them._ I'd ra - ther see the

star.   Our   dia - monds are e -
sky.   Our   sap - phires are stu -

- nor - mous but she'd ra - ther see a
- pen - dous but she'd ra - ther see the

star.   Our   Cer - ber - us has
sky.

three heads, yes three heads, yes

three heads. Our Cer - ber - us has

three heads, up - on my word And

each of them barks loud - er far than

a - ny dog you've heard. You

really - ly ought to hear___ him. Woof

woof, woof woof, woof woof, woof woof_ I'd

ra - ther hear a bird. Our

Cer - ber - us has three heads but she'd

ra - ther hear a bird.

The Sun, the Sun, the Sun

Who turns the night in - to day? The

sun! The sun! The sun!

Who turns the grass in - to hay? The

sun! The sun! The sun!

Who in Hea - ven do you sup - pose

melts all the dew drops on the rose?

About the Author

Julia Donaldson is the author of some of the world's best-loved children's books, including modern classics *The Gruffalo* and *The Gruffalo's Child*, *The Snail and the Whale* and the *What the Ladybird Heard* adventures. Julia also writes fiction, including the Princess Mirror-Belle books illustrated by Lydia Monks, as well as poems, plays and songs – and her brilliant live shows are always in demand. She was Children's Laureate 2011–13 and has been honoured with a CBE for Services to Literature. Julia lives in Sussex with two tabby cats.

About the Illustrator

Kate Pankhurst lives in Leeds with her family and spotty dog, Olive. She has a studio based in an old spinning mill where she writes and illustrates children's books. Recent projects have included the Fantastically Great Women series and Mariella Mystery Investigates series.

Kate is distantly related to the suffragette Emmeline Pankhurst, something that has been an influence on the type of books she enjoys creating for children.